S

Volume 2

Mark Cassell

C000082418

DISCLAIMER: "This is a work of fiction. Names, characters, places and incidents are products of the author's imagination and are used fictitiously. Any resemblance to actual events, locales or persons, living or dead, is entirely coincidental."

Copyright © 2023 Red Cape Publishing

Copyright © Mark Cassell

All rights reserved.

Acknowledgements

RIVER OF NINE TAILS - Originally published in *In Darkness, Delight: Creatures of the Night* anthology by Corpus Press, 2019.

REANIMATION CHANNEL - Originally published in *The Black Room Manuscripts Vol.4* anthology by The Sinister Horror Company, 2018.

SANTA'S ELITE - Originally published in *The Horror Collection: White Edition* anthology by KJK Publishing, 2019.

HACKED (co-written with Patrick R. McDonough) - Originally published in *Shallow Waters Vol.3* anthology by Crystal Lake Publishing, 2019.

THE INCIDENT AT TRENT HOME - Originally published in *Broken, Battered Bodies* anthology by Matt Shaw Publications, 2021.

THE THING INSIDE - Previously unreleased companion story for the novel *Parasite Crop* by Caffeine Nights Publishing, 2021.

DEDICATION

This one's for Adam.

Thanks for being you, bro!

Table of Contents

River of Nine Tails

"Any idea what killed him?" the American shouted over the chugging engine.

Elliot couldn't answer, couldn't drag his eyes away from the dead Vietnamese guide. The boat rocked as he watched the other man shuffle along the wooden seat and clamber over their rucksacks, ducking beneath the branch that had torn the canopy. In all his thirty-eight years on the planet – indeed, hardly ever leaving England and observing the world vicariously through either the TV or Google – this was only the second dead body Elliot had seen. The first had been his wife.

"Where's the kill switch on this thing?" The other man's lip curled as he stretched over the body to reach for the engine.

Smoke belched from the long vessel's exhaust, filling the blue sky with grey clouds.

As the only passengers on the sampan, the first they'd known of any problem was when the canopy ripped, and the boat thumped the riverbank. Elliot's immediate thought had been that they were stopping despite the lack of a jetty and the captain had misjudged a landing.

The American, whose name Elliot didn't actually know, cut off the engine. He scrambled backwards, awkwardly manoeuvring around the slumped body, and the silence of the Mekong Delta closed in.

For the first time on his round-the-world travels, Elliot wanted to go home.

"Look at that mess." The man's voice seemed even louder now. "Look!"

Elliot *was* looking.

The Vietnamese man who'd introduced himself as Captain Duc, wore brown trousers and an open shirt. Blood glistened on dark skin from where it dribbled over his chin and down his neck. Dead eyes stared through the remaining smoky wisps, seeming to fix on the relentless sun.

The boat tilted as the American stood, his sunglasses swaying on the cord around his neck. "It's leaking!"

Brown water lapped his sandals, splashing his socks. Blood swirled.

"Stand still!" Elliot yelled and grabbed the wooden rail. "Seriously, mate, don't move."

"I can't swim."

When Elliot relaxed his grip, he slowly stood, bracing himself against the rocking motion.

"We're in the shallows," he said, now standing straight, "we'll be absolutely fine."

Again, the other man shifted sideways. This time the sampan tilted.

"Whoa!" Elliot yelled.

Duc's body flipped to sprawl facedown, half over the side. A limp arm slapped the water.

"Jesus, what the fuck?" the American shouted.

"Keep still!"

Two ragged, near-circular holes of flesh and shirt fabric gaped beneath the dead man's shoulder blade. There were even a couple of ribs on show, splintered, grisly.

"What could've done that?" the man demanded.

Water rapidly filled the boat, now lapping their shins.

"Eels?" Elliot murmured, but doubted his words. "Piranha?"

He knew he was talking bollocks; he had no idea what the hell could've done it.

The man's chest heaved. He looked about ready to have a panic attack. Elliot's own breathing was fast. Beside him, extending almost parallel with the torn canopy, a low branch hooked out over the riverbank as though offering assistance.

"Come on," he said, and reached for the branch.

Water splashed as the American headed for Elliot, and the boat jerked to the left and right.

"Slowly!" Elliot shouted before he could gauge the branch's strength.

The water level rose and sploshed around them, covering their knees in frothy bubbles.

"We must get off the boat!" The man flailed arms, the boat rocking. He barely managed to keep upright. The rails were sub-merging and the shredded canopy draped into the water. He slipped, yelled something, and leapt toward the riverbank.

Elliot looked up to the branch and allowed it to take his weight.

Behind him, he heard a splash and water drenched him. Waves rushed the mud and tree roots that lined the bank, and the boat pulled away from his dangling boots. For a moment he hung there, then hoisted himself hand over hand along the branch; awkward yet successful, he finally tiptoed the muddy bank and dropped to his knees. With his breath coming in short, hot bursts, he scrambled through reeds and slick foliage. Mud squelched.

"I'm soaked," came the voice beside him.

Mud covered the other man's clothes, mostly caking his lower-half, so much so that it looked like he wore brown trousers. His hair was flat to his scalp and water dripped from a stubbly chin. Despite the situation, Elliot almost laughed. Humour was his defence mechanism, and this was the kind of moment where it would erupt as uncontrollable laughter. Instead, he used Duc's floating body as a way of sobering him up.

It worked.

"We need to get out of here," he said.

The American's jaw flexed as he scooped mud from his clothes, while behind him the sampan sank lower, levelling with churned blood and froth. Duc's body, a water bottle and a plastic bag drifted downstream, chased by swirling bubbles to disappear behind tall reeds where the river narrowed.

"Whatever killed him," Elliot said, "could still be in the water."

"Dude, stop stating the obvious."

"You have any idea where we are?"

"Do I look Vietnamese?"

"Mate, I'm only asking."

They stood on the riverbank and watched the waves lessen, giving way to ripples which rolled out toward the opposite bank.

"Brandon."

"Huh?" Elliot looked down at the outstretched hand. "Oh, right, yeah…" He clasped it. "Elliot."

Although Brandon's grip was all mud and water, it was firm, friendly. "I don't mean to be a dick."

"I get it." Elliot wiped his now-muddy hand on his shirt. "That was enough to make anyone lose their cool."

Brandon motioned to the river. "My phone was in that rucksack."

"Want to dive in and get it?"

"No chance."

"I've not had a phone since I left the UK," Elliot said, wondering when precisely he'd disconnected from the world. It hadn't been when he cancelled his phone contract, it was way before that. The months leading up to his departure blurred as though he'd sidestepped reality, so perhaps that was the reason why he felt somewhat desensitised to the insanity around him right now. He knew he should be scared shitless, wearing a similar wide-eyed what-the-fuck-has-just-happened expression as—

Brandon was still talking. "... and you're a rare one, buddy. The first traveller I've met who hasn't been glued to a cell phone. New experiences for these youngsters, and they're all attached to those things. No hope for mankind's future. Eventually everyone will live life vicariously through a screen."

Elliot glanced around them. He had no idea what to do. Perhaps there was a small part of him that wanted to wade out into the water, search the murky depths and confront whatever it was that had killed Duc. Maybe the animal had answers about Death.

"I figure," Brandon continued, "we are both older than your typical traveller."

Elliot blinked, shivered, and focused on the man's words.

"Yeah, I guess," he murmured.

He too had met countless other travellers, most in their late-teens or early twenties. They had no idea how life could set fire to your balls. Whether boy or girl (not *man* or *woman,* they were just kids after all), they'd often exchange short conversations before they returned to a handheld device, hunched, squinting. Granted, some were searching online for information about their surroundings, local traditions, translations, and the like, yet the majority seemed fixated with that constant need for validation from peers on the other side of the globe. In the twenty-first century, there was no longer a round-the-world trip, it was more a round-the-world ego-trip. There would always be that lifeline back home for them, certainly, but there's no absolute freedom of being let off the leash, to absorb each and every experience at hand.

A lifeline… For Elliot, besides parents both in their seventies, he had nothing left back home. Not even a house. Not anymore.

And now he didn't even have a spare pair of pants.

Brandon pointed to the brown depths of the Mekong Delta. His voice echoed on the hot air as he yelled, "How the fuck did that man die?"

***

Keeping the winding length of the river to their right, the two men agreed to follow its course, where eventually it would lead them to My Tho, the village in which they boarded the sampan. Not wanting to walk too close to the water, knowing what lurked beneath its brown depths, they kept it just in sight.

After a long stretch of silence, soon Brandon

asked, "What brings you out here?"

Elliot wasn't ready to answer that, especially to a travel companion whom he'd met only a few hours ago. Thoughts of Jane immediately came to him, albeit fleeting, yet enough for a familiar icy hold to grip his stomach and rise to his heart. Loss, guilt, confusion. Loneliness. He almost said, "To escape" but managed to catch himself and instead replied, "To see more of the world."

Seeming content with that answer, Brandon nodded enough to make it necessary to push his sunglasses back along the bridge of his nose.

They walked in silence again.

"The Vietnamese refer to the Mekong Delta as 'Song Cuu Long', or something like that," Brandon eventually said, "and is over two-thousand-seven-hundred miles long."

"Yep, and it starts way up in eastern Tibet."

"It does."

Elliot stopped and looked over the other man's shoulder to where he could just about see the river through swaying palm fronds.

"Apparently, Song Cuu Long means 'River of Nine Tails.'"

Elliot didn't answer, he stared at the river, thinking he'd seen something.

"Or maybe it's 'River of Nine Dragons'," Brandon added, mistaking Elliot's attention on the river for interest in his trivia. "I can't remember now. I read it some—"

"Shhh."

The fronds steadied, making Elliot wonder if they'd moved because of the current or something else. He couldn't hear anything. He stretched his neck, not wanting to approach in case that something else was there.

"What's that?" he whispered.

Brandon turned to look, his jawline twitching and eyes bulging behind sunglasses.

A gnarled branch broke the water's surface.

Elliot started to laugh, relax, then—

It was not a branch.

Whatever Brandon said next was snatched by a torrent of water and parting fronds. In a rush of scaly limbs and a blur of mud, what appeared to be an alligator or crocodile (Elliot had never known the difference) scrambled up the riverbank. Toward them.

The thing had the body of a crocodile yet had no mouth, just a long snout with a splintered stump where a horn once was. As the men staggered backwards, sideways, yelling and sliding in the mud themselves, Elliot failed to work out where the torso ended and where its limbs began. Limbs... too many... all along its back, thrashed and whipped away branches and foliage. Whatever the animal, this *creature*, was, it lashed out with those determined appendages – that's what they were: appendages with snapping mouths, like tentacles only with glistening circular maws filled with yellow teeth that lined the throats all the way downwards.

Such was the insane moment, Elliot somehow managed to count the fucking things. Nine. Nine thrashing appendages, not including the four stumpy legs, each ending in claws as long as his forearm.

"Run!" he shouted and sprinted up an

embankment, further into the jungle.

"What the fuck is it?" Brandon's voice was too far behind.

A glance over a shoulder, and Elliot saw the man had only just made it onto the embankment. He scrambled clumsily in the mud as though his legs disobeyed him. He got up, threw a wide-eyed glance at the lumbering animal, and ran toward Elliot. At least, he tried.

He slipped sideways and whacked the ground with a "Hummmph!"

From where Elliot stood, flanked by looming trees, he could see only the top half of the man…

There was a slapping sound like a wetsuit dropped onto soft sand, and a crunch. Brandon screamed, and his head and shoulders fell from sight.

More wet sounds, more crunching…

Elliot went to take a step toward the poor bastard – he had to help! – but then saw a whipping appendage, bloody, slick, glistening in the rays of sunlight which lanced from the jungle ceiling.

More screams…

From somewhere far away, yet perhaps closer than Elliot thought, something like a horn blew. A piercing note, shrill. It seemed even the birds silenced as well as Brandon's screams. Then another note. The same, only this time sustained.

Something thumped and a branch snapped.

"You run, motherfucker!" Brandon shouted.

The horn's blast silenced in time with a great splash. Out on the river, water misted the air like a thousand sun-glinting crystals.

Brandon groaned, and Elliot ran to him.

He huddled in the mud and wet leaves, clutching his leg.

Elliot moved in beside him, marvelling at how the man wasn't yelling. Bite marks, unsurprisingly identical to Duc's, covered his leg from thigh to ankle. One was ragged and to the bone. Blood streaked his skin, saturated his sock and dripped on the ground.

"Mate," Elliot whispered.

His first thought was a bandage for the worst of the wounds, and so immediately unbuttoned his shirt and shrugged out of it. Ripping fabric always looked easy in a movie but as he tried, he slipped and smacked his hand on the tree beside them.

Now Brandon began whining.

"You'll be fine, mate." Although Elliot wasn't entirely certain. All the shit he learnt back in school, and they never taught him to deal with a man whose leg had been ravaged by a river monster with nine mouths. Algebra, long-shore drift, how Jonas Salk cured polio in 1953... but what do you do when faced with a wound such as this?

The man now mumbled while Elliot succeeded in ripping the arm off the shirt. The tearing sound seemed too loud. Perhaps the creature would hear it and come back. This time for him. A squint through the foliage, at the now-still Mekong water, revealed nothing.

Somewhere far away a bird cawed.

He calmed his breathing, if only for Brandon's sake, and wrapped the fabric around the ravaged flesh.

"That's the worst of them," he said and gave it a

final pull.

Brandon hissed through clenched teeth. Spit sprayed.

"Not sure what to do about these bite marks, though."

"It hurts, man!"

"Now who's stating the obvious?" Elliot looked at the remains of his shirt, not caring he was now topless. It was wet, covered in mud with leaves and twigs sticking to it, but it would have to do. He tied it around the man's leg as best he could.

"Thanks."

"You're going to be fine," Elliot assured him. "You reckon you can walk?"

"I sure as fuck don't want to stay here."

The jungle buzzed with insects, something Elliot hadn't noticed. Now the adrenaline had lessened, and blood no longer roared in his ears, he guessed it made sense that he'd begin to notice their surroundings.

"Let's get you up," he said and offered his hand.

The buzzing sound seemed to be getting louder. Closer.

Brandon looked past Elliot's bloody hand. "Is that...?" His voice was hopeful. He shifted in the mud and winced, placing both hands on the ground ready to push himself up.

"A motorbike, yeah."

"Scooter." The American still didn't grab his hand. "Two of them."

Elliot lowered his arm and followed the man's gaze to peer deeper into the jungle.

It was indeed two scooters revving, and eventually

they weaved through the jungle and fully into view. Both riders were young men, one whose open shirt flapped behind him, and the other who wore a red cap. As they approached, they exchanged something in rapid Vietnamese. They pulled up in a burst of engine revs and churned mud, not too far away.

"Thank God," Brandon said, now clutching his leg again. He'd settled back down.

A cloud of petrol fumes clung to the air as the two riders regarded them for a moment.

The man with the open shirt dismounted and kicked out the stand. Around his neck was what looked like a dried chili looped through a rusty metal ring and tied to a twisted leather cord. Elliot guessed it was some kind of Vietnamese superstition; back in the UK, it was a rabbit's foot for a lucky charm, so why not a chili?

The guy with the red cap stayed mounted.

"Thank God," Brandon said again as Chili-Man crouched beside him.

"You guys speak English?" Elliot asked.

Red Cap looked at him, then at Brandon.

"No?" Elliot pointed to the wounded man. "He needs help."

"Yeah, I need help." He hissed as Chili-Man prodded the makeshift bandage. "Hey, hey! Gentle! Come on…"

Chili-Man looked up at his companion and said something.

Elliot had so far visited Thailand and Cambodia, and while exploring, he'd made every effort to learn pleasantries: hello, goodbye, please, thank you, plus other useful words. Sometimes even phrases. Now, faced with this emergency – let alone the fact that their guide had earlier been killed by a river monster – he wished he'd invested in something as simple as a phrase book. However, even if he had one, it would no doubt be at the bottom of the river.

He had to accept this insane situation they faced.

Red Cap finally dismounted from his scooter and wheeled it up against the foliage. His dark eyes fixed on Brandon, then he said something so rapidly, Elliot doubted if he understood even a little of the language, he'd fail to catch it. Although, perhaps he heard the words "Cuu Long."

"Hospital?" Elliot asked. "Um, medic, medicine… pharmaceutical… nurse?"

Chili-Man pulled out a hunting knife.

And thrust it into Brandon's chest.

"What the—?" Elliot's words echoed around them.

Brandon's eyes bulged, looking at the blade slide out from the gushing wound.

Elliot stepped forward. Someone from behind – Red Cap, of course – grabbed his arms. He wrestled in the man's grip while he watched Brandon's head fall back, dead eyes locked on the branches overhead. What felt like rubber pinched his skin, binding his wrists. He struggled, uselessly.

"Get off me!"

Chili-Man approached him, slowly raising the dripping knife. Perhaps a smile twitched his lips.

"Don't do this!" Elliot yelled.

A fist swung upwards and Elliot's nose exploded in a hot wet crunch. In a blur of tears and motion, the two men forced him to his knees.

"Mnnnnnnn, mnnnnnn, mnnnph," Elliot said through a weird suffocation.

They crammed something green into his mouth, something bitter. Clamping his teeth together and trying to breathe through a broken nose was impossible. He tried to spit the stuff out, but they rubbed it over his teeth and gums. It tingled.

The pair laughed and released him.

With his arms bound, he thrashed about in the mud, spitting, choking.

"Bastards," he said, but his voice sounded strange. Perhaps... perhaps it was... because... his nose... broken...

Stones and twigs and leaves scratched his naked torso, yet it all felt somehow distant... too far...

And a darkness crept into his vision.

Pressing in, sideways, numbing. A coldness spread through his body, and all he could taste was that bitterness.

With an ankle each, the two men dragged him past the body of his brief and now dead companion. He slid through mud, trying to kick, to struggle, but his body didn't seem to obey.

That darkness came at him in waves.

As the drug took effect, tangled thoughts battered him. He wanted to laugh about the fact that he'd only just learned of the American's name. With his brain whirling, his face on fire, he squinted through tears and blood and that pulsing blackness, and Elliot said goodbye to Brandon. Silently though, because now his lips didn't – *couldn't* – move.

By the time they had him beside the river, his arms and legs were utterly useless. Paralysed, it seemed, apart from his brain… yet even that was as slow as the river's current, that gently lapped his boots.

They left him there.

Alone… to be fed to that creature…

Don't leave me!

Elliot listened to the two Vietnamese men return to their motorcycles, mud squelching and twigs snapping. One engine sputtered, revved, and then the other. Both now revving, they rode off.

Hey!

Engines faded into the silence.

Hey!

Now he was left with only the sound of the Mekong Delta.

As he lay there, feeling the sunshine on his face in that disconnected sort of way, the realisation that Death was coming comforted him. Perhaps he was ready… He'd seen Death up close. Three times now: Twice here in Vietnam, the other back home in the UK.

Jane…

Death wasn't too far away, and this time it was for him. If there was an afterlife, he'd get to see his wife again.

Did… did something splash just then?

Jane.

Why was it, when Death approaches – now in the guise of the thing that had killed Captain Duc – you begin to question if there's some other place beyond all this?

Maybe something did splash.

This was it.

Time to die, Elliot.

And he was happy to accept.

He closed his eyes and thoughts of Jane soaked into him as even now he knew the mud and water soaked into his clothes. Of everything about her, all that she was… and – Death was coming, right now, just for him, all for him – and how he'd rushed her to hospital and… and not long after that how the surgeon's well-practiced apologetic gaze fixed on him, and—

Splosh. The sound of a rowing boat.

Jane?

A boat.

Was he relieved? Perhaps, perhaps not. What was his life now?

A slim wooden canoe cut through the water's surface like a knife spreading smooth peanut butter on bread.

He wondered if his saviour had any food on board his vessel.

Help me.

The small man with a conical hat guided the canoe toward him.

Hunger pangs – he felt *them*. Yet still he couldn't feel his legs. Or arms.

Did he want to call out? Did he actually want to be saved? Death, for Elliot, was not quite ready for him after all.

Jane, maybe I won't be joining you. Not yet.

***

Twilight pressed in on the darker greens which

flanked his journey, the rhythmic splosh and creak mesmerising, almost hypnotic. Elliot was sprawled in the canoe, looking up at his conical-hat-wearing saviour who rocked back and forth, heaving the oars up and down, splosh and creak, in and out of the water. The man was perhaps in his forties, a fisherman Elliot assumed, given the tangle of net and rope that he now laid on.

He was still hungry, and the sky was darkening.

Perhaps the man was taking him to a fish farm, and he'd be fed one of Vietnam's tasty dishes. What was the fish called? Elephant ears, of all things. Yes, that was it…

Definitely hungry now.

Elliot's nose was still blocked, and so he breathed through his mouth. Also, just like his arms and legs, his voice failed him; he wanted to thank the man, wanted to talk about what he'd witnessed. Regardless of whether or not the man understood English, Elliot *had* to tell him.

He had no idea what the hell it was they'd shoved in his mouth, but at least the effects seemed to be wearing off. The numbness had subsided, and he felt the humidity of the evening, plus the wooden boards beneath him poking into his back. Still he couldn't move, but he guessed it wouldn't be too long before he'd regain control of his body.

This was all insane.

Occasionally, his saviour would look down at him, flashing a brown-toothed smile. Mostly though, he'd glance over his shoulder to keep the canoe on course to wherever their destination was.

Stilted wooden houses lined the water's edge,

their crooked jetties clawing out from the riverbank. The aroma of cooking meat teased his swollen nostrils, while the occasional local man, woman and child stared through glassless windows. At one point, where the river narrowed, a group of children sat on the riverbank and whispered among themselves. One girl, whose dress seemed too bright for her surroundings, pointed to the canoe as it sent ripples toward her bare feet. Her toes curled, and she giggled, nudging the little boy beside her. He grinned.

Elliot wanted to wave... but couldn't. Although his fingers did manage a pathetic twitch.

As he passed, not wanting to lose sight of them, he craned his neck – or indeed, he *tried*. Too much effort. As he returned his gaze upwards, to the first stars now piercing the ever-darkening sky, he felt the children's eyes follow him.

The canoe cut its way through the winding river, taking him deeper into the Mekong Delta. He wondered where their destination would be. The man's home? And how long until they reached it?

The sky darkened further. He had no idea how long he'd been in the canoe, nor did he have any idea how much time had passed since seeing the children. Or how long it had been since the men on scooters, and... bloody hell, they'd killed Brandon. And what about the river monster?

Elliot's breath quickened.

Eventually the sky turned to black and unknown constellations stretched overhead, sharp, bright.

On his twelfth birthday, Elliot had unwrapped a telescope after months of pestering his mum and dad for one. He'd already learnt every constellation in the Northern Hemisphere and so wanted something to take him higher into the night's sky. With light pollution diluting the skies where he grew up in the UK, here in Vietnam, it was the blackest he'd ever seen. Beautiful. Inspiring, no less. And he saw every star, millions of them, sparkling.

Truly remarkable.

Listening to the rhythmic splosh and creak of the oars, and looking up at those unknown constellations, he wondered what had made him lose interest in astronomy. He'd never thought of it before now, but he guessed it was the following teenage years that did it. He wondered whatever happened to his telescope. Perhaps it was still in his parents' attic. Also, come the age of fifteen and sixteen, he'd developed a huge interest in music and soon learnt to play guitar. Then—

"Sex, drugs and rock'n'roll," he said in a nasally voice. Chili-Man had done a fine job of busting his nose.

The Vietnamese man glanced at him.

Something shot past the man's shoulder. A fiery streak.

At first, Elliot thought it was a shooting-star, but another fired past him. This time from the other direction.

Fire. Yes, that was it.

Another, and another.

Fireflies.

So many.

Those fireflies reflected the constellations, and in seconds, more filled the sky as though they intended to stitch a canopy between him and the blackness. Thoughts of a canopy led to thoughts of the sampan and Duc. The river monster. Brandon. The hunting knife. Death. And Jane.

Always, thoughts of Jane were never far off…

Watching the fireflies' intricate pattern weave overhead, by the time Elliot noticed the rhythmic splosh of oars had ceased, something filled his mouth. Fingers. A bitterness caked his tongue.

Tingling…

***

At some point, Elliot must've lost consciousness. Or at least he'd kept floating in and out of lucidity. When he opened his eyes to squint into a sunrise, he couldn't quite make out where he was. With arms and legs awkwardly bound, pinching his skin, his muscles numb but no longer in that drugged way, it felt as though he was tied to a tree. Although, the surface was smooth: concrete, a pillar of some kind.

His head banged with the mother of all hangovers. Even more than the one the day after Jane's funeral. Indeed, he thought *that* had been up there with one of his greats.

From somewhere close by, flies buzzed. His nose was clogged, and it felt ten times larger than it should be, yet still the smell of damp concrete invaded his heavy head. A foul taste filled his mouth.

He was in a building, in a single room featuring several rows of pillars that reached up to a broken roof. Sunlight pushed through the overhead gaps and through the barred windows to his left and right, enough to spotlight dozens of rotted cacao husks across cracked tiles. In places, the tiles had given way to sprouting weeds and heaps of dirt. The main exit, not too far ahead of him, was nothing more than a rectangular hole in the wall which probably once framed double doors. Crumbled steps led down onto grass that stretched a short way into tall palm fronds and reeds, and then the river. Brown, still, all-too familiar.

He could not recollect how he'd got there. He remembered that bitter taste and a sickness filling his head. He remembered being wheeled into the jungle – on a cart, yes, pushed by the man he'd mistakenly thought of as his saviour. He remembered seeing more Vietnamese locals, mostly adults this time, solemnly watching him. He remembered how the ride was jerky, a constant nausea repeatedly stealing him into a private darkness.

His ears were ringing, a fuzziness still pressing into his mind, thoughts colliding. It threatened to again snatch him into blackness. His chin kept bouncing back onto his chest. It was such an effort to lift his head, so he kept his eyes down, staring at the filthy tiles. What looked like rubber tubing was bound tight around his bare ankles. Close to his muddy toes, absurdly, was a grubby playing card: the three of diamonds. There was no sign of the rest of the deck.

He'd been stripped down to his underwear, and he shivered despite the humidity. Feeling incredibly vulnerable, he almost screamed yet managed to catch it before it tumbled from dry lips. What if the monster was nearby? He didn't want to attract any attention, not wanting the monster to know where he was. He knew, however, that the monster would probably be able to smell him.

And speaking of smells... what the hell was that *other* stink clawing down his throat? It was putrid. He lifted his head, albeit slightly, and squinted into the shadows. Huddled in the corner, flies buzzing around them, he saw several heaped bodies. Mostly naked, each with similar wounds as he'd seen on Duc's body and Brandon's leg. He shifted to the left and right, and saw, then heard, the others in the building with him.

A sound outside, from behind, made him twist awkwardly, trying to look over his shoulder.

With his eyes now adjusting to the building's gloom, he saw he was far from alone. It appeared he was one of eight men and women, all stripped down to their underwear, all bound to a pillar. Listening to the surrounding whimpers, he was surprised he'd not noticed his company any sooner. His ears were still ringing, though, so maybe that was why.

Bound to the opposite pillar, a dark-haired woman, perhaps in her fifties and wearing mismatched underwear, hung with her head down. A long stream of spit dangled from quivering lips.

Elliot awkwardly changed position, so he could see the others, the rubber tubing pinching his wrists and ankles.

There was an unconscious man whose black skin hid beneath so much mud. He'd puked down his chest and it had spattered the broken tiles at his feet. Another man, Asian and wearing boxer shorts covered in smiley faces, was murmuring to himself, his eyes glazed. There were two women, neither any older than twenty, dressed in bikinis. Daylight streamed through an adjacent window to highlight lank hair clumped over sunburnt and blistered shoulders. One was unconscious, her chin on her chest, while the other murmured, her eyes rolling behind flickering eyelids. A mumbling older man with hair thick with dry mud, glanced at him and shouted something in German (Elliot understood some of the language, but not whatever it was that came from his blood-flecked lips). Although bound to the nearest pillar, he couldn't hear what the German then began to mumble. The other captives he couldn't quite see, so didn't know whether they were male or female; he only saw their silhouettes in the gloom. However, he knew they too were all in a similar state of either confusion or drugged oblivion.

More shuffling from behind.

Someone else, a young guy wearing blue swimming shorts, was being dragged into the building by two men. His eyelids flickered, his lips trembled. Elliot was not surprised to recognise his captors: Chili-Man and Red Cap.

"What do you want from us?" someone screamed, the words echoing in the confines of the building. Such was the voice that shrieked, it was difficult to tell whether it was male or female.

From a ragged throat, Elliot shouted, "What is this?" and coughed.

No one answered.

A woman yelled: "Let us go!"

Again, there was no answer.

The German continued mumbling without even

lifting his head.

As the two men went about tying their final captive to a pillar, another man entered the building. Vietnamese like the others, although much older, he was bare from the waist up, his skin wrinkled and saggy. He held a curved horn in both grubby hands. Hollow, etched with curious sigils and symbols, it balanced on his palms as though precious.

"No, don't," Elliot murmured. He remembered the last time he'd heard the horn being blown and it made the creature return to the river. So he could only assume this time it would summon the thing. "This is madness!"

Chili-Man and Red Cap stepped back from the newly-bound captive whose head now lolled. A long stream of spit dribbled from his chin. They walked away, footsteps echoing, and passed the older man. They nodded to him. He didn't acknowledge them as they left, simply continued into the centre of the building.

"Don't do this!" Elliot shouted.

"Please, let me go," someone whimpered in what sounded like a French accent.

"Let us all go!" shouted someone else.

The German still mumbled.

Now holding the horn in one hand, the old man raised it to his lips, inhaled, and blew. Given the confines of the room, the note it played resonated, filling Elliot's head.

The old man blew again, long and loud.

And another, and then another.

"Stop that!" Elliot yelled.

Someone else: "Please!"

The dark-haired woman shrieked: "Noooo!"

Something splashed in the river.

Everyone hushed, apart from the mumbling German.

Elliot's heartbeat filled his head. Death was finally coming. Coming for them all.

He squinted through the exit and out toward the river. There was more splashing, and branches cracked. Palm fronds swayed. There... there was the mouthless snout of the creature. The ivory stump on its forehead glistened, trickling water.

Those who saw the creature screamed.

The creature lumbered up the bank, its reptilian bulk sliding through mud, and those vile appendages parting and breaking fronds. Emerging fully into the daylight, the creature paused and hung its head, nostrils flaring as though seeking something.

Us, thought Elliot, *it's following our scent, our fear*.

In an almost-casual way, it dragged its fat body toward the building, head low to the ground, those appendages thrashing the tall grass.

More screams echoed.

As the first paw reached the cracked paving slabs, the appendages calmed, yet still the mouths chattered. It heaved itself up the steps. Claws scraped and clicked the broken masonry. Its snout twitched, its head swayed. Even slower now, it slithered into the shadows and headed for the bodies in the corner.

The screams lessened, becoming sobs and curses and whispers of denial.

Flies scattered as the abomination slumped against the pile of dead, to nestle into the embrace of bloated limbs and rotted flesh. Curses quietened to whimpers, and Elliot swallowed his fear the best he could. Perhaps the monster wasn't going to feast on them after all. The appendages jerked, mouths closing one by one. Each coiled in on itself, some wrapping around another, tightening against the thing's scaly flank. It reminded him of Medusa's hair.

Without any sign of the horn-blower, a strange silence fell upon the captives, interrupted only by rhythmic panicked breathing and the occasional sob.

The thing didn't move, seeming content with its bed of dead bodies. Its black eyes closed, and eventually flies began to settle on its flank and unmoving appendages. The only movement now was its gently flaring nostrils. Softly breathing, its bloated stomach extended and contracted, extended and contracted. And—

The mud-streaked stomach split in a mess of blood and oozing filth, steam rising, curling into the shadows.

And three eggs, each as large as a man's head, spat out.

***

The monster, this abomination of nature, shuddered. The grotesque appendages shivered, and the mouths chattered, briefly, then silenced. Its tail cradled the three ovoid eggs. Filth streaked each mottled shell, glistening weakly in the poor light. A stench of rotten fish and seaweed wafted through the building.

Someone gagged, heaved, and Elliot heard vomit spatter the floor.

A convulsion wracked the creature's body and a front claw stretched to clutch the tiles, and then the other. Still its eyes were closed, and with steaming offal flopping out of its split gut, the creature began to drag itself away from the eggs. The tail uncoiled from around them and slid through the muck. The appendages were still intertwined close to the creature's spine and several of the mouths opened and closed. It was as though they gasped.

Screams and yells erupted. Elliot, too, added to the cacophony, his throat raw as he and his fellow captives, those lucid enough, watched the creature manoeuvre away from the eggs. Blood and filth smeared the tiles in its wake, claws scraping.

Elliot struggled in his bonds, bile rising in his throat. Reaching the centre of the building, the creature slowed and then eventually slumped as though its legs gave out. He saw the stump at the centre of its head and knew that the horn that was once there became the tool with which to summon it.

He eyed the eggs. Why had they captured him and the others? Were they to be food for the eggs once they hatched?

A man shouted, "Let us go!"

The creature appeared to be dying, its nostrils flaring, its head twitching. As it inhaled and exhaled its final breaths, the appendages unravelled, mouths gulping air.

One detached with a squelch. Sentient. It slopped on the floor.

Another, and another. They left only raw holes

along the creature's back, oozing pus and watery blood. In seconds, the nine appendages snaked lethargically away from the creature's now-still form. One by one, they slithered away, each in separate directions. Blind, weaving through the detritus across the floor…

The captives quietened, a collective intake of breath to share a blanket of silence.

Each snake-thing wriggled, seeking, teeth chattering…

One reached the German first. He no longer muttered. It teased his feet, and if anything, he looked more curious than fearful.

Another flopped, writhing in dirt and slime, approaching someone else further in the shadows. Elliot couldn't see who it was.

Further away in the corner, highlighted by streaming sunlight through a hole in the roof, Elliot saw one squirm toward a woman. As if with a sudden surge of life, it coiled up her leg. She shrieked. Trailing muck, the thing reached her face, teeth chattering a million miles per hour. In less than a second there was nothing left of her skin other than a ragged mess. Her scream was silenced when it shot down her throat, tail vanishing. She gagged, choked, convulsed.

So far none had approached Elliot, nor the unconscious dark-haired woman opposite, but he knew it was only a matter of time. He looked about him, searching for nearby movement.

He saw nothing. Yet.

The German didn't move as he simply allowed the snake-thing to reach his chest, its teeth grinding. His own mouth wide, he jabbed his head forward and bit down on it. He shook it from side to side, blood and muck misting the air. It thrashed in his jaws, snapping its teeth, trying to gain purchase on his chest or shoulder or neck or… It clamped onto his nipple and tore away a flap of skin and chunk of muscle. He yelled, releasing the thing from his mouth. It darted for the wound, ribs snapped. Blood sprayed as it punctured his heart. He contorted, and his head dropped. The snake-thing burrowed into his chest, but slowly, its tail whipping spasmodically. Then it flopped and hung from the gaping wound, evidently dead.

Another poised in front of a young woman, coiling down into itself, ready to pounce. She screamed at it, bucking and twisting. It sprung upwards and dived into her mouth. She choked, writhing. Then she was still.

Yet another did the same, this time to the Asian man. Gurgling, choking, and thrashing.

Close by, something slurped. Elliot jerked around, looking for—

A snake-thing leapt up on him, slimy, warm, wrapping its tail around his shoulder and armpit… then his face. It smothered him, and corkscrewed around his neck, strangling. Dots peppered his vision. Desperate to keep his mouth closed, he struggled beneath its slippery length. His nostrils hissed through busted cartilage and bone.

No choice, he gasped…

The thing jammed into his mouth.

His throat stretched as it forced its way downwards. Utter agony.

Darkness closed in… and with it, unconsciousness.

***

In a myriad of colours, greens and browns, and the colour of Death, Elliot's vision shifted into bright light. His heart beat a monstrous rhythm in a tight chest. His sore throat felt like he'd swallowed a melon, and his stomach was bloated, aching as though he had indeed consumed one. He wanted to spew.

Then he remembered: he'd swallowed one of those fucking snake-things.

His breath started to come in sharp, short, painful bursts.

Moonlight pressed in through the barred windows and broken roof. From what he could tell, the other captives, those who remained, were slumped, unmoving. A dark filth puddled at their feet. Someone remained bound to a pillar, the man's stomach and chest ravaged like a sack of meat, sliced and gaping. A snake-thing lay folded in the bloody mess near his feet, dead. Another was on the floor a little farther away. Several were coiled, motionless in the shadows. And the eggs… they were still in the corner against the dead bodies.

Some of the other victims had evidently been removed from the building and it appeared there were only three people left alive, himself included. Still bound to the pillar opposite, the dark-haired woman squirmed. The whites of her eyes shone beneath fluttering eyelids.

A fiery pain exploded in Elliot's gut and snatched him back into the dark. Head spinning, the blackness welcoming. A brightness, a darkness, together it churned.

Within a peculiar half-light, half-dark, someone approached…

Footsteps echoed. Perhaps there were even voices.

Elliot's mind whirled, a sickness washing over him, smothered in stink. He looked around, scanned the slumped bodies in the shadows. The woman gazed at him, her jaw slack, her eyes reflecting little more than pain and confusion. Her lips parted as though about to say something, but instead belched. The stink blended with the taste in his own mouth. His stomach rumbled. His fingers tingled. A heat filled him, moved within, and a rush of nausea buzzed like insects.

Again, darkness took him back down, down, down… As the buzzing sound seemed to intensify, the churning darkness melded with the light.

Someone pinched his chin, calloused fingers rasping on stubble.

"Huh?" he shook his jaw away from the fingers.

Through the darkness and flashes of sunlight, a wrinkled Vietnamese face squinted through the shadows which again threatened to take Elliot down. It was the old man from earlier, however long ago it had been when this bastard summoned the monster: the horn-blower. It was as though the man was inspecting him.

Most of the other pillars were now empty. Rope and rubber tubing coiled in puddles of clumped meat and blood and motionless snake-things. The dark-haired woman was still there. Blood and spit dribbled from her lips.

She screamed, and the sound snatched him upright.

His stomach twisted. Agony. Interchangeable, dark and light, shadows and sunshine... and maybe this time there was some motion.

He felt his arms and legs released, and his body slumped. His knees cracked on the floor, palms slapping the cool tiles. Two more men approached: Chili-Man and Red Cap. They lifted him, each man hooking one of Elliot's arms around their neck.

Malnourished, his head heavy after being drugged, he pathetically wrestled with them. But they effortlessly dragged him out into the daylight where the sun burned. It was as though his fists were made of rubber.

In moments they reached the riverbank.

Were they now going to let him die here?

Blinking into the sunshine, the water teased his feet as the two men left him alone. Movement from beside him, and he noticed the woman was also slumped on the riverbank, their unbound legs tangled in reeds, their bodies sprawled in mud. The sun burned his bare skin, made him itch. The sound of the men retreated back into the jungle, back toward the building.

He tried to call to them, but he only succeeded in dribbling.

The woman shivered, clutching her distended stomach.

He, too, rubbed his stomach. It looked like he was pregnant. Looking at the woman who faced away from him, for a moment he thought she was his wife... but images of the monster, the building, the eggs, the snake-things, consumed him. She was not his wife, she was not Jane.

Had they been freed?

Yet... yet inside him there was no freedom. Inside, that *thing* was there.

He moved, slid through mud, his fingers caressing something slick, curved.

An egg.

The woman shifted to face him. She belched. The stink was foul. She already held one of the eggs, but the shell was lighter than his. Just the two of them there, huddled in the reeds at the water's edge, both like expectant parents. Why was the shell of her egg lighter than the one he held? Something was wrong. Inside: no life. The egg, dead. For a moment, he remembered... something... someone... Jane. His Jane... They'd conceived. They were once close to being parents.

He pressed his face to the eggshell. It cracked as he pushed his hairy chin into the goo that oozed through segments of shell and tearing membrane. He didn't much care for the taste; he didn't much care for anything now.

Once, though, he *did* care.

Mouth open, he buried his face in the muck and slurped the gloopy contents. As he did so, he thought of Jane and the child they never had, the life they never had, and the life Jane lost. The life, the *lives*, he lost.

The woman reached out for him, her fingers raking the blistered, crusty skin of his arm. Her mouth opened, and she murmured something, then coughed. Her body shook, then was stolen by convulsions. The egg rolled beneath her. She arched her back and turned over and crushed the egg with her bulbous stomach. Spasms wracked her body, and calmed, and then she was still.

He stared into the woman's dead eyes.

Time seemed to stretch, the sun arcing overhead, changing from hot to warm. Eventually the sun vanished. While the first stars pricked the darkening sky, he realised he clutched an egg. It nestled between his thighs. He could not remember how this last egg, this healthy egg, had got there.

His egg.

He closed his eyes, accepting the darkness.

Only this time it was a content sleep.

***

Waves gently lapped him. He felt different. His breathing moved like liquid, as though valves opened and closed somewhere in his throat, his nose. He slid into the mud and lowered himself into the welcoming depths of the Mekong Delta, watching his hands cup the brown water. A glance behind, and he saw the egg almost glow under the burning red of sunrise.

The woman's body, grey and sun-scorched, now hid beneath a haze of buzzing flies.

He felt a sheen of translucent skin shift over his eyeballs as he submerged. Beneath the water, he could see perfectly. He swam and marvelled at the tiny bubbles tracing the scales that covered his arms.

Beneath the water, he glided. Agile. Powerful.

Along his back and shoulders there was a mild discomfort, and he felt movement there. It was the extra appendages that were even now splitting the skin down his spine.

He would not swim out too far, nor for too long.

He couldn't.

He could not leave the nest.

Soon, he headed effortlessly back toward the egg cradled in the twists of broken fronds. His head broke the surface, water tumbling down his long face. The sun was now higher, burning orange through the reeds where the egg was barely visible. As he waded closer, he saw a crack appear in the ovoid shell.

He slid through the mud, keeping the egg in sight.

The shell cracked further, fragments peeling. A scaly muzzle tore through the thin membrane as though sniffing the air. A frail claw reached out.

The thing that was once Elliot embraced its child.

Reanimation Channel

The front door to his neighbour's house was open when Scott got there. It offered a narrow strip of vertical gloom between splintered wood.

"Adrian?" he called.

Moonlight pressed his shadow into chipped paintwork. He stuffed the Royal Mail missed-parcel card into a pocket, then nudged the door inwards. The broken lock and cracked frame snagged his coat as he stepped into the man's home. A stink of leftover food, mildew, and something else filled his lungs. Such contrast to the salty breeze coming off the coast.

He manoeuvred around crumpled beer cans and at least a dozen torn pizza delivery boxes. Busted furniture and shredded upholstery should have made him call the police. But he didn't.

"Adrian?" he called again, this time louder.

The *other* smell that stuffed itself down his throat was animal, though he wasn't aware the man had any pets. Whenever Scott returned home from work after Adrian kindly signing for a parcel, his neighbour always gave the impression of not wanting visitors. The pair would always exchange small talk, and Adrian was never rude, it was just that sometimes when pressed for more, he seemed distant.

This was the first time Scott had entered his home.

He tiptoed between the ruined furniture. Maybe Adrian was an untidy kind of guy, sure, yet his place looked like it had been burgled. However, there was something more going on.

That *smell*.

Scott's parcel, the typical manila-coloured cube he associated with the CD boxsets he often ordered, rested against a scuffed chair leg. He ignored it and moved towards the threshold to the next room. More pizza boxes and drink cans littered the floor of what was the dining room (the house was a similar layout to Scott's). This was evidently dedicated to his computer rather than somewhere to formally eat. Adrian once used the term *computer station*, and on seeing it, Scott understood why. It proved to be an old-school set up, consisting of an upright unit beside a flat-screen monitor with its red standby light glowing. In front of which, a classic keyboard and mouse huddled between heaped crisp wrappers and snaking cables. A set of headphones dangled over the desktop edge.

In the shadows under the desk, a mobile phone sat against the wheel of an overturned swivel chair.

Two more cautious steps forward and—

Beyond the splintered dining-room table, Adrian lay slumped against the carpeted staircase. He'd tucked himself into a foetal position like a scared child.

A sour taste filled Scott's mouth.

The man's dead eyes stared at the ceiling. Blood pooled – so dark, almost black – and it framed him in streaks up the wall.

Seeing that, his first dead body, washed a rush of emotions over him. Confusion, horror, disgust, sadness. Even a mortality-check. He wanted to back away… he wanted to clamber over the buckled table to somehow resuscitate him… he wanted to call the police, an ambulance, a fucking fire engine.

He didn't know what to do.

Adrian had not curled into a foetal position.

A coldness scratched the back of Scott's neck, and his feet seemed to sink into the carpet, the fibres clutching his boots, pulling him into the floor.

He wanted to run.

Where Adrian's legs should've been, there was only a pair of bloody stumps. Bone shards glistened between shreds of flesh and jean material. Whatever did that to him had not cut them off. They'd been torn off.

Scott's stomach churned. That smell filled his head.

Slow motion, back and forth, his gaze drifted between the computer desk and the man's body. He felt his lips working but nothing came out. Reaching sideways, his hand shaking, he clutched the desktop. As he stared at his white knuckles, he recalled a conversation they had on the doorstep, perhaps only a few days ago...

Typical of any summer evening despite the heat of the day, the coastal breeze chilled him as he thanked Adrian for taking in his parcel.

"No problem," his neighbour said, looking down at Scott. "You know I'm always in, and I don't care how late you knock."

Scott glanced at his watch: it was almost ten o'clock. It had been a long day in the office, and he hadn't realised that was the time. "Sorry, mate."

"Seriously, I hardly sleep." He shrugged. "Insomnia."

"I do appreciate it.' He took the package from Adrian's long fingers. "You okay?"

"I'm good." He pulled the door behind him, blocking off the view into his lounge. "I think."

Scott looked at the man's unkempt hair, his creased T-shirt. "You sure?"

For a moment silence stretched between them, then Adrian said, "How's the world of fraud investigation?"

"It's getting worse, mate."

"Yeah?"

"The internet has a lot to answer for."

"You can never be too careful, huh? In fact..." He pulled the door even closer behind him. "...I've signed up to a new game."

"Cool." Games didn't interest Scott but he decided not to voice that.

"At least," Adrian added, "I've put in a bid."

"Nice. Well, good luck in winning." He guessed he spoke of eBay or something. Scott had never been a gamer. Music had always been his thing, and he was the first to admit that most of his deliveries were CDs. He was traditional when it came to music: give him something tangible rather than a list of faceless MP3 files.

Now, still clutching the desk, with his other hand Scott tapped the spacebar on the keyboard. The screen brightened, making him squint.

The website and application – the *game* – Adrian had been on was one often thrown around the office: Reanimation Channel. It existed on the dark web. When working in fraud investigation, it was vital to know about the multi-layers of the internet. From what Scott understood, subscribers to this channel could bid on the chance to control what was essentially a reanimated animal. And they were never small bids put down. Often *thousands* of pounds. The user could watch via a live feed from an action camera strapped to the thing's head and control its every move. The freaky science behind it was beyond him but as far as he could tell, it was similar to how years ago engineers in the US developed a way to control cockroaches by hardwiring miniature computers into the insects' nervous systems.

He remembered thinking when first hearing of this insane advancement in technology, such practices could not end well.

For his neighbour here, clearly it had not.

He had to call the police and leave it up to them. His fingerprints were already dotted around the place, and this was not a time to start playing with evidence. So far Reanimation Channel had kept under the authorities' radar – essentially the joy of the dark web – and there were of course many moralistic questions thrown up with this crazy "game".

With Adrian's mutilated body huddled in the corner, Scott knew how utterly stupid it was as curiosity forced him to click on the live-feed window. For a second or two nothing happened, and then the video pixelated into motion.

"What the hell?" he whispered.

The video feed revealed a narrow pathway lined with foliage beneath the dark blue expanse of a cloudless sky. Moonlight occasionally flickered in the periphery. The area wasn't too far: it was a route he sometimes used to head down to the promenade and onto the pier.

But... but it was the upturned hand flexing hairy

fingers that made his skin cold. Whoever – no, despite those almost-human hands, this was *what*ever – wore the action camera, rubbed blood between thumb and forefinger.

Scott had no idea how Reanimation Channel actually worked, but he was certain this should not happen. For the reanimated animal to escape, Adrian must have somehow lost control. However long ago since his death, there could now be many more lying dead in this creature's wake. A creature, sure, not an animal. This was way beyond anything he'd heard in the office.

"What are you?" he asked the screen.

The live-feed shook, the hand dropping out of sight, and his view panned first to the left and then to the right. More trees.

What was it doing now?

Onscreen, alongside the feed window, a number of parameters swept up and down in rainbow waves. They reminded him of the graphic equaliser on his first Hi-Fi back in the 80s. Beside these parameters was some kind of controller, with arrows pointing up, down, left, right, and the appropriate diagonals in between. Beside these was an array of buttons, each sporting various symbols and acronyms. He had no idea what any of them meant. Until that moment, several had been flashing, and now the creature had stopped, only a couple remained blinking. He assumed these were the control buttons, the ones Adrian had paid God-only-knew-how-much to have access to. And to what end? What had he wanted to do? Why would anyone want to control such a creature?

"Who's been controlling you since you left here?"

Again, the feed jerked, and this time offered a view of the pathway behind the creature, from where it had come.

The heavy air of the room caught in Scott's throat. Could the thing hear him?

He snatched up the headphones and slipped them on his head. Both Adrian and Scott had the same sized skull. The sound of laboured breath rasped in his ears. That, and the ocean wind hammering the trees. A quick scan of Adrian's computer station revealed there wasn't a microphone.

"Can you hear me?"

Again, the feed swung round, this time going full circle. A low rumble sounded, evidently the creature grunted.

"This isn't coincidence."

Another grunt.

No microphone... Telepathy? Absurd. There had to be a microphone.

The feed shook as the creature darted sideways, away from the path. Shadows and moonlight flashed as it bounded through the undergrowth. It issued a growl, low and throaty. Heavy footfalls thumped the ground, and branches whipped its body. Occasionally the claws came into view, and soon the beast staggered out into a grass clearing. A view of the ocean spread out in the distance, moon and stars reflecting from the dark expanse. For that time of night, Scott wasn't surprised to see several people along the promenade. Some in groups, others alone, and of course plenty of couples walked hand in hand.

Time to call the police.

Yet still he stared at the screen.

Someone screamed. With the headphones clamped to his head, the sound blasted through his brain. He grimaced. Then a dog barked, franticly.

Up ahead, the silhouette of a woman in an over-sized duffle coat shone her torch at the creature. The beam burned into the feed to make the image flash in a crazy bright whorl. It settled, sharpened and Scott watched as the creature rushed forward. Hairy arms reached out to shove the woman. She fell and screamed again.

The torch lay in the grass a short way from her, spotlighting the barking terrier beside her. Saliva flew in the air.

The creature bent down to stare into the dog's face.

One more bark, and it stopped, lowered its head, and backed off. The woman still screamed, scrambling backwards, now pulling at the dog lead.

Scott dug in a pocket for his phone. Was there a blue light from somewhere? Skirting the periphery of the camera feed, something blue definitely flashed. The police were approaching, thank God.

All he could assume was the creature had regained control of itself and was now acting entirely of its own free will. This opened up a whole tonne of questions. How had the creature become self-aware? No one controlled it, so how had that happened? Or was someone controlling it after all?

This wasn't his business. He had to get out of the house and wait for the police.

The dog mewled. Repressed, somehow.

In a blur, the creature leapt at the woman. Given

the action camera's placement, Scott watched as her face twisted in agony. Her scream filled Scott's headset. The blue light was a bizarre kind of electricity or energy that traced the creature's arms as it ravaged her. The sound of the creature's laboured breath intensified as the woman's clothes shredded. Chunks of skin slapped the ground out of sight, and gore filled the camera feed...

Why the hell was he still watching this?

He fumbled for his phone as the creature backed off.

The woman's body lay sprawled on the grass, now just a tangled mess of duffle coat and twisted limbs, raw and glistening red. The dog nudged the woman's blood-caked hair.

Almost like a drum, a rhythmic beat started up, soft at first but getting louder, stronger. The live-feed shuddered and the view of the woman's remains shrank as the creature soared in to the air.

The dog began barking again, though the shrill noise faded the higher the creature rose.

Velocity. Wind and thumping wings filled the headphones. With such speed, trees and gardens, cars and houses rushed below.

A giddiness washed over Scott.

This was insane.

Behind him, not from the headphones but from the back of Adrian's house, something crashed. Shattering glass, crumbling masonry, and a bestial roar...

Scott turned, and—

The cloying stink of wet animal wafted over him.

A hairy fist swung through the air and hot pain

exploded in his face. He staggered backwards into the computer station. The monitor slid off the desk and smashed to the floor.

With his nose on fire and blood filling his mouth, he scrambled into a sitting position. His head reeled.

The creature towered over him, its chest heaving.

Whoever was behind Reanimation Channel had created a Frankenstein monstrosity of what seemed to be part-human, part-dog, and... part-bird?

Scott choked on the heavy coppery taste in his mouth and an icy fear overcame him. Certainly, the thing had once been a man, he saw that. Beneath the patchy hair and feathers, the flesh glistened, sweaty and slick with its victims' blood. Wires and circuits wove through swollen flesh. Its head was a mess of what was perhaps a German Shepherd fused with a bearded man. A twist of coloured wires bulged at its temple and where the dog's ear should've been, Scott saw a curved metal plate. It reminded him of the chrome exoskeleton of the Terminator, only not as shiny. This was a monster beyond anything he'd ever seen. Secured to the head, horrifyingly absurd, was the action camera. Traces of the blue energy trickled along the exposed circuitry.

Veiny membranous wings extended behind its torso, creaking and clicking. Made of bone and cartilage woven with feathers and mottled skin – stitched with what looked like clothing – they reached outwards, spanning the room.

Scott clutched his nose, blood streaming between his fingers. His heartbeat was as loud as his breathing. He had to run. Now. But fear still froze him, dizziness clogging his thoughts.

He realised the bones were in fact legs… A glance to the body of his neighbour confirmed it. It had used the poor guy's legs to create those grotesque wings. Blue flashes of energy traced their expanse, flowing along the veins. The tech that crowned its head blinked LEDs.

Its eyes, dead and black, half-hidden in circuitry, stared at him.

Scott's forehead prickled with sweat.

The thing growled and folded its wings out of sight.

A quick glance around and Scott saw nothing with which to protect himself. Useless debris littered the floor; crisp packets and pizza boxes, energy drink cans and all kinds of rubbish. Although the dining table was broken in two, nothing was suitable to use as a weapon. He pushed further back, his face throbbing. It felt like he had a hot, wet sponge behind his face.

The creature stepped forwards. Plastic casing of a stereo system cracked beneath its weight. Slick with mud and leaves, those long feet were hairy.

He was a dead man if he didn't find a weapon. His head swam, and for a moment a darkness threatened to snatch him away.

The creature stopped, hunched, yet not like it was about to pounce, more as though it was confused. Its head jerked left and right, and slightly tilted.

Pressed up against the computer station, Scott was ready to bolt.

Clumsily it manoeuvred around the furniture and crouched beside Adrian's body. It reached for his head. Within the stitched circuitry of its forearm blue light pulsed. Hooked fingers caressed the man's cheek, then lowered to clamp the shoulder. Bones crunched. Stringy gristle, sinew and ragged flesh stretched, and with a final crack, the entire arm came away.

Scott suppressed a yell, not wanting to draw the creature's attention. All he could do was press himself into the tight space under the desk. He knew there was no easy escape should the creature come at him.

But he didn't want to budge.

The creature pushed the floppy limb into its own arm, and the hair bristled, parted. The skin beneath rippled and moulded with the human skin like it was clay. Traceries of that blue electricity linked the patches together. Sporadic feathers stood erect.

Scott clamped his lips together, feeling a bile rise up his throat.

He watched as the creature pulled off Adrian's other arm, and went about the same moulding, twinning of flesh. He squinted into the intensifying blue light, mesmerised as it bulked itself out using Adrian's torso. A sickening wet and crunching sound echoed around the room as flesh and circuit and bone stitched together. Clothing, too.

Now the creature was a mess of feathers and skin, deformed and out of proportion with a small head, snouted and sporting a halo of circuitry. Such was the extent of chaotic fusing, the action camera was almost hidden beneath folds of skin and fur.

Day to day, Scott dealt with fraud in the safety of an office cubicle. Witnessing this kind of shit was beyond anything he could ever have imagined. He was now dealing with a monster constructed of technology and corpses. Heartbeat loud, his face on fire, for the first time in his adult life, he wanted to curl up and cry.

From somewhere far away, an engine roared. A car, a truck? No it wasn't, it was an aeroplane, low in the sky. Perhaps even a helicopter. Yes, that rhythmic throb of rotor blades was unmistakable. Close. Maybe overhead.

He hoped, he prayed that whatever vehicle it was, was piloted by someone who was going to save him from this insanity. Again, he felt a darkness creep into his vision, pressing in on all sides as he watched the creature flex new muscles.

With gnarled toes curled in a pool of blood, it shuffled forwards. Towards him. Both arms, one more defined than the other, reached for him.

Scott went to crawl out from beneath the desk, but that would get him closer to the creature. He had nowhere to—

The creature stopped, fingers twitching. Then nothing. A dull clicking sound came from somewhere as though there was a conflict of mechanisms. Even the blue light faded, remaining only along the circuits in its skull.

A red light pulsed, then that, too, faded.

The deformed head jerked like it was confused. Its eyes closed.

Had someone finally taken control? Quite possibly. Or perhaps it had taken on too much and the circuits couldn't manage.

Its eyes shot open, black pupils locking onto him. It issued another growl which became a shriek to tear through his brain. He cupped his ears with blood-slick hands.

Again, it closed its eyes. The shriek cut off.

Its heaving chest rippled; one last patch absorbing what Scott assumed was a part of Adrian's ribcage.

Blue light flared again, blinding. The creature's back straightened, and those impressive wings shot outwards. One punched into a wall, plaster and brick crumbling. They retracted once again. It stumbled one way, then the other, arms outstretched, clutching for him... and lunged.

Scott recoiled and the back of his head smacked the wall. Powering through his thighs, he thrust upwards. The desk shifted as he leapt sideways. Everything clattered to the floor, and in a tangle of cables he emerged.

The creature straddled the debris, still reaching out. Closer, closer...

He went to run and—

A clammy hand gripped his forearm.

He yelled, waited for the crunch, waited for the agony of bones breaking... but a sudden silence fell on him. He tried to pull away. Couldn't. Even the creature's breathing had reduced. Again, its eyes were shut.

The thing had frozen... with Scott's hand still in its grip.

He pulled again, with no success. He couldn't release himself. With his other hand, he gripped his wrist and tugged. It didn't give, not even a little. Panic filled his throat, breath rasping. Every gasp was filled with a heavy animal stench.

Still the creature did not move.

This close to the thing, breathing in that fetid odour, he saw the intricacies of stitched flesh and feather, of fabric and fur. In places, bone had fused with circuitry and wire, and where everything had moulded together, a yellowish pus oozed, dribbling and clogging thickets of hair and pimples.

The corner of the snout twitched, flashing stubby grey teeth. The tech along its scalp glowed blue.

He yanked again.

"Come on!" he shouted.

The creature's eyes cracked open... and focused on him.

Pain exploded in a horrible crunch as his bones were crushed. He yelled and black spots dotted his vision – this was not the time to lose consciousness. If he did, then this thing would wrench off his body parts.

Another ear-splitting scream dribbled from its mouth. It stuttered to a halt, jerking and flailing its free arm.

Then it let go of him and he fell to the floor. A sickness boiled in his stomach as again a coppery taste filled his mouth. He swallowed another mouthful of blood, coughed and straightened. His useless arm flopped, and tears blurred his vision.

The creature stumbled.

More dizziness swept over him. He cradled his arm, limp and mangled. For an absurd moment as the creature stomped around the room, flailing its limbs and spitting grunts, he wondered how he'd explain things at the hospital – if he ever got out of this.

Again, the creature staggered forward. Its eyes flared, tiny and glowing with an inner fire. And that damned camera strapped to its head, blinked. Like a third eye, it watched him.

On unresponsive legs, he struggled into a sitting position. He realised he was humming something, some tune. Then he wondered where his package was. Then remembered: he'd seen it earlier. He knew his parcel was in the lounge, so he shuffled towards the archway between rooms. He clutched his busted arm to his chest. Pain came at him in waves. He didn't want to die. Not yet. He never even got to tell anyone what tune he wanted at his funeral. He didn't want anything generic or commercial, he wanted something punchy, rocky, meaningful to him, his life, to who he had been… He wasn't ready to die.

He pushed himself to his knees. He had to get up. He'd only knocked on his neighbour's door for his parcel.

The creature growled, now ignoring him.

Something out in the kitchen smashed and clattered.

Was that the back door?

The sound of boots echoed through the agony that roared between his ears.

A darkness peppered his vision, and although he was already close to the floor – so far away from his parcel – gravity lowered his reeling vision closer to the debris-strewn carpet. Beside him… beside… him… so close… was the creature…

He wanted his parcel.

The thing dropped with a floor-shaking crash, sprawling across the remains of the dining table. Its black eyes stared – dead? – up at the swinging lampshade overhead.

Scott again pushed himself up, still hugging his useless arm. Nausea twisted in his stomach, clogged his throat. And maybe... maybe he saw that blue lightning tease his crushed arm.

"No," he muttered. "Please, no..."

A slow crawl to the other room... slow... painful... and eventually he reached the parcel... tore it open with only one hand, marvelling at his dexterity.

Voices from out in the kitchen. Shouts. One female, one male. The female yelling, commanding.

His vision swam, floating in and out of focus.

"No!" he shouted, holding the CD boxset in a blood-slick hand. "This is not... what... I ordered."

He couldn't believe this was happening. All this, and they'd delivered the wrong... fucking... CDs. Darkness and agony began stealing him away.

When heavy footfalls reached him, a familiar blue electricity traced the bone shards that stuck through the skin of his forearm.

"I didn't... want... this," he mumbled to the woman who stood over him. A sensation of pins and needles washed through him.

The boxset fell from numbed fingers.

As the pain faded, his vision shrank.

Within the embracing silence, he saw the attractive lady in a trouser suit frown at a handheld device. She prodded it while saying something to her colleague. The man beside her was also well-dressed, like a security guard. He clutched an automatic weapon, pointing the barrel directly into Scott's face.

Finally, as a numbness swamped him, the silence, the darkness, folded in. Complete.

***

Scott came to amid the rhythm of an engine. Darkness. And music. It was as though he climbed from a dream – which it must've been, surely? Perhaps he recognised the tune that now thumped around him. Something restricted his arms and legs, and through a peculiar numbed pain, he realised he was restrained. Where was he?

There was something about the sound of the engine, something he recognised. Like the music. That tune…

Much he recognised, but for the numbness.

His eyelids cracked open, and a dim light forced itself into his head. Along with a paralysing claustrophobia.

The engine. That rhythm.

Was he in a helicopter?

Confusion, a crashing of memories… Listening to that rhythm, that music, he remembered being squashed in a crowd. The music thumping around him, beating, hammering his teenage brain. Mesmerised by the mad throng of people surrounding him, squeezing him in, tight.

That was how he felt right now. Closed in, *boxed* in.

He'd never been in a helicopter. This was the first time. How did he get here? His vision sharpened and he saw his confines: secured behind glass. The curved panel reflected the light of—

Yes, a helicopter. One of those large cargo helicopters with tandem-rotor blades.

Maybe even military.

Clarity poured over him, albeit briefly. Perhaps Reanimation Channel was in fact a military project. His thoughts collided, and his senses tangled. A dizziness squeezed his brain.

From somewhere far away, yet not that far, was the music. From the cockpit he assumed, and just as suspected, he recognised the tune. If he really listened, somewhere in his head, probing his memories, he recognised it... Confusion. And memories. He was back at his first concert. With his dad. But... he could not quite remember which band or artist it had been. Back in the early nineties, certainly. But who was it? The tune drilled into his head, diluted by other memories. As he concentrated, trying to push away the dull pain that wriggled through his body, he wanted to laugh.

This was a dream, right?

A laugh bubbled up his throat.

He tried to move. Couldn't. His wrists and ankles were strapped to a rigid cradle. Coloured lights flickered in his periphery. His view was of the curved interior of a helicopter, and the back of a woman's head. She hunched over a computer terminal. He recognised her, yet from where?

Strapped to a wooden pallet which in turn was strapped to the metal rungs of the floor, a large plastic container towered over her. Blood streaked the panels. Scott thought that he should know what it contained, but he couldn't... think... straight...

The music blended with the pulse of the aircraft's engine.

He twisted and failed to see anything else. Even

his head was secured. He willed himself to stretch, to reach a hand further than his restraints allowed... and his forearm thinned, unnaturally... like his bones were made of clay. He couldn't do it with his bad arm – a probing memory wanted to remind him what happened.

Still the woman faced away from him, now with headphones pressed to an ear.

He managed to snatch his hand from the harness. A tingling sensation climbed up his forearm and into his shoulder. He felt his body fuse with the plastic cradle.

A familiar blue light sparked across his vision.

Where had he seen that before?

The glass misted with his breath, and he pressed his palm against it. His skin stretched, linking his fingers like webbing, and he saw his bones silhouetted. They, too, transformed. A crack echoed.

And he saw the woman – he recognised her, but from where? – spin round to look at him.

Her eyes widened.

She dropped the headset.

Ran towards him.

The cradle blended with him, and he spread the flesh and bones of his clay-like body... he became one with the metal, the plastic...

The woman reached him, her mouth moving. Whatever she yelled was lost in the tune which he still couldn't recall. What was it, dammit?

He extended his body, pushing through the glass casing to embrace her, to pull her into him, to blend their bodies. Her clothes and skin and bone, everything, became a part of *him*. More extension, more expansion, his very *being* flowed outwards, now entwining with parts of the helicopter.

Then...

Then he merged with the floor, reaching the plastic container that housed the remains of the thing that started all this. The dead creature, once again reanimated as he moulded with those chimera parts. The container also became a part of him. So, too, the pallet beneath, every nail and splinter.

Soon, he connected with the hull of the helicopter, every rivet and panel and wiring and circuit became his body.

Next, it was the instruments.

The engine hum changed pitch.

Someone in the cockpit yelled. A man staggered out, holding a handgun.

The thing that was once Scott snatched the man into himself... *itself*. The weapon, the ammunition, everything fused. The surging energy which pulsed within the body of fused material, overcame the helicopter.

The tandem-engines stuttered to a halt.

Descent.

New to this body, the entity failed to control the machine.

Gravity snatched it. Wind whistling, mechanics groaning. Down. Down...

A cold sea swallowed it in a rush of waves and froth and dark depths.

***

A mid-morning sunshine reflected off the English

Channel in a sparkling expanse dotted with the occasional fishing trawler. Above the sharp horizon, a cloudless sky stretched from west to east. The pebbled beach, before it levelled out into sand and lapping waves, was mostly hidden beneath sweaty bathers on rainbow-coloured towels. Shielded by fortresses of windbreaks and umbrellas, children played while parents squinted at phones, magazines, books, or simply lay motionless with eyes closed.

Smoke drifted where typically pot-bellied men hunched over portable barbeques. Couples walked hand in hand along the water's edge while dozens of swimmers bobbed in the water. Some children, keeping to the shallows, played with inflatables.

The promenade teamed with bustling families, through which runners and cyclists, and skateboarders alike, zigzagged. Sunlight glared from windscreens in the car park adjacent to the seafront.

Further along the beach, Hastings pier crawled into the sea like a centipede with metal legs. Its wooden body jagged with multi-coloured huts which offered everything from ice creams and T-shirts to trinkets and palm-reading.

Wherever possible, seagulls scavenged pebbles, boards and pavements for food. Their cries shrill, matching the joyous shouts of children, to pierce the hum of traffic.

Music pumped from speakers at the core of teenagers slumped across benches. A blue-haired girl who wore studded boots and a long coat surely too heavy for this weather, nudged her boyfriend. They shared an equal number of face piercings and the same taste in black clothes.

She pointed.

The others in her group looked up.

Out to sea, far from where the boldest of swimmers rose on the waves, something had emerged from the water's surface. Something dark, perhaps metallic... yet, not quite.

With the music loud, none of the teenagers heard the grinding noise that rumbled beneath thrashing waves.

However, those on the beach and nearer the water could hear.

That's when people shouted.

This *something* which later people would find hard to describe, slid through the bubbling rise, froth splashing. Seaweed clung from its uneven bulk as it rose like a giant blister. Its limbs, if they could indeed be labelled as such, were malformed and twisted, awkwardly extending like tentacles. The thing sloshed and rushed for the shoreline, pushing a tsunami to those paddling in the shallows. The glinting tentacles shot outwards. Another, and another.

That's when the screams began...

The thing was a monstrosity beyond what witnesses would soon be calling a giant octopus or squid. Its flesh did not have the sheen of any typical cephalopod, rather it was an insane fusion of metal and plastic, driftwood and machinery, pebbles and cockles, fur and flesh – not just human flesh, but that of varying species of mammal including dolphins, sharks, and whales. An absolute abomination of nature.

More screams.

Everyone ran.

Great waves crashed the shore, slamming people into the sand and pebbles, sending them sprawling over one another.

Screams echoed.

Countless tentacles, stitched with the same patchwork materials as the body, arced high overhead, spearing sunbathers and snatching them up. Arms and legs flailed, blood misted the air while towels and debris hurtled into the fleeing crowd.

People sprawled, trampled.

The thing slithered from the water, that grinding sound ever-louder. Fatter tentacles clutched at the sand, burrowing deep to drag its body fully into the sunshine. It had no discernible shape: just a hulk of quivering gelatinous flesh made of gore and junk.

The creature's prehensile limbs whipped the beach, coiling around those unlucky enough to be in its path. More and more people were absorbed as well as food coolers, umbrellas, deck chairs. *Everything* fused into that bloated monstrosity. The more flexible, smaller feelers lingered around music players and speakers, toying with them. These, too, were swallowed into the rippling flesh; earphones and headphones, cables and all kinds of electrical equipment vanished into its bulk.

Soon, in the distance, sirens could be heard. Not that the emergency services would be able to do much by the time they arrived.

Seemingly content with that which it had absorbed, one last tentacle snatched up the speakers that still pumped out music. The teenagers had long-since fled.

The creature retreated.

It slithered through the remaining detritus. Pebbles and debris shifted, clacking and clicking under its weight. From deep within its body, something thrummed, a constant rhythm. A heartbeat? That was anyone's guess. It headed for the sea, leaving this part of the beach in chaos and ruin.

Pink, frothy waves welcomed the grotesque creature…

Submerging, sliding beneath the waves, it manoeuvred itself away from the shore, further into the sea. Eventually nothing could be seen of it. Later, someone across the Channel, someone on a fishing trawler or ocean liner, will no doubt spot it.

By the time it reaches France it shall be much, much larger.

Santa's Elite

Here amid the ranks of what are known as 'Santa's Little Helpers' we each have a story to tell. Most speak of their desire to make children smile (yeah, that old chestnut), for others it's the ability to construct presents parallel to those sold in stores (talent), and there are of course the guys involved with the alchemy behind Santa's magic (that stuff goes way over my head!). Everyone has an origins story, just like any superhero.

However, for some of us it's because Big Red is struggling with his workload. We're the Elite, Santa's Secret Service so secret all the other departments are oblivious to our year-round missions.

You see, 100 years ago Earth's population was around 2 billion, and now pushes 8. It grows by an estimated 74 million per year and sprints towards 10 billion – a total which scientists claim is the Earth's maximum capacity for resources as well as comfortable living. That's supposed to come about in only 30 or 40 years from now, so just think how Big Red must feel? That's a shit-tonne of work every Christmas Eve. His magic only stretches so far, you know.

The world is gonna get pretty damn cramped if nothing's done about it.

That's where Santa's Elite comes in.

Before I get to the crack of it all and tell you what the Elite actually does, I should explain things from when I was a husband living in the UK with a wife who loved TV, chips, and chocolate, way more than she did me. I guess my catalyst was when France's Notre Dame cathedral burned. There was much more to it but while my ignorance at the time allowed me a short-sighted view, all I saw was that within 24 hours something like half a billion euros were pledged for restoration. No one died in that fire. Whereas back here in the UK, about 50 families remained unhoused from a tower block fire two years previous in which 64 people died.

We were one of those families.

When the fire ravaged our tower block, my wife and I were sitting in a shitty café down the street arguing about her infidelity… all the while my parents burned to death. Needless to say, the following two years were absolute hell. During which time she had another affair – the one of which I knew, at least. Please don't ask why I remained with her because I simply do not know. As pathetic as it is to say, I was scared to be alone and knew nothing and no one else.

When the Elite recruited me, my eyes were immediately opened. Wide. Trust me, it isn't climate change we have to worry about, it's the Earth's doomed population. Up here in the North Pole it's still rigid with ice mountains – incidentally, I *love* my big duffle coat. But that's not my point.

The world is fucked, and the Elite are working all year round to save your arses. Well, those of you who've stayed off the Naughty List (yep, that really is a thing).

So, let's first talk about Christmas Eve of 2019, the day my life changed.

***

The kitchen was so small I had to shoulder closed the door, disconnecting myself from Kathy's domain just so I could open the oven. With the drone of the TV now a muffled Christmas tune of which I could never remember the name, the roar of the electric fan filled the room. Heat swept over me, but it smelled lovely.

We were still living in our temporary accommodation two years after our possessions became ash in the tower block fire.

"Kathy?" It was perhaps the first time I'd spoken all day. Wearing oven gloves that barely succeeded in their job, I placed the covered dish in the centre of our wobbly table. "Food's ready!"

I set out a pair of chipped plates on either side of the dish and laid the mismatched cutlery. Just as I sat myself down, the door creaked open and my wife ambled into the room. Her familiar unwashed odour drifted towards me. Often it was from one extreme to the other, where she'd either reek of cheap perfume or stink of days' old sweat; there was never a pleasant in-between. She settled into the chair opposite, grunting. I removed the lid from the dish, allowing steam to billow as though the meal sighed. The meat and vegetables, the teasing heat, the aroma of those herbs I'd mixed with the gravy, was in fact pleasing.

Her voice shot across the table. "Not eating that."

She may as well have punched me.

As if to clarify, she added, "There's veg in it and everything."

I shrank.

There was more: "I'll eat the meat though."

I clenched my teeth to restrain the scream that clawed up my throat.

Keep your eyes down, I told myself, *keep them down, don't look up. Serve yourself, there's more for you if she doesn't want it.*

My fingers curled around the serving spoon.

Pressure from above, overhead and beyond that cramped kitchen as though our bed pressed through the bare floorboards, through the cracked ceiling and grimy light fitting. I wanted to hide beneath the table. To cry – but I never did. At least, never in front of this woman I shouldn't have married.

I inhaled the aroma as if it could blanket my deadened excitement – I was in fact annoyed at myself for even thinking she may enjoy the meal. Why did I occasionally bother to make something other than sausages, beans, and chips? Seriously, why? If it wasn't loaded with the ingredients for heart disease, diabetes, or cholesterol, she wasn't interested.

With the greatest of effort, I straightened up in my chair. The wood pressed awkwardly into my spine.

Kathy began chewing, loudly.

My efforts now washed away, it was like someone else's hand lifted the serving spoon to scoop the vegetables and meat. My plate, piled. Her plate, pathetic: just meat. I spied the green flecks of herbs and was surprised she didn't moan about that.

With a remarkably steady hand I picked up my fork, the one with a crooked prong. Then a knife (this one was at least straight). The sound of Kathy's wet mouthfuls drifted towards me, sliding across my skin to rake the back of my neck. My knife sliced through the meat, gravy oozing. Like mud. Using the knife, I pushed the vegetables up against the meat, and raised the loaded fork to my mouth.

In it went.

There was nothing wrong with it. It was pretty good, but... I glanced at Kathy. Her eyes were fixed on her meat-filled plate. Yeah, it looked like mud. A ruined meal, unappreciated. Why did I even bother cooking anything?

As it often was since hell's fire snatched away the pathetic life we had, only to make it even more pathetic, the meal was eaten in silence.

Mouthful after mouthful, Christmas Eve dragged on.

Eventually, Kathy's knife and fork clattered on the plate.

I looked up, waiting for her to leave the table, to shuffle off without a word and return to the lounge, to get back to whatever brain-numbing shit she'd been watching. A furrow creased her brow for a lightning second, and her lips parted as though to say something. She licked her lips, her tongue catching a herb that stuck to the corner of her mouth.

I lowered my gaze to my plate and continued the last few mouthfuls.

Her chair juddered on the linoleum floor and she grunted, then jerked upright. She stood, eyes rolling, and swayed as a strange silence filled the tiny kitchen. She dropped to her knees and her chin smacked the table edge. Her head snapped backwards. Plates and cutlery rattled.

And she sprawled across the floor.

I slowly got up from my chair, wiping my mouth with a sleeve.

The doorbell clanged, echoing from the lounge. Still to this day, I have no idea how I knew it was one of Santa's Little Helpers come to rescue me.

I simply *knew*.

Although the TV volume was cranked up, Mariah Carey singing about what she wanted for Christmas sounded muffled – I absolutely detest that tune. Every year it's everywhere! Don't even get me started on the fact that the other departments insist on playing the entire fucking album. Luckily, I don't often tread their offices; we Elite spend most of the time travelling around the globe.

When I pulled the front door until the chain went taut, cold air rushed in as a dishevelled face peered up through the gap. He had to be no more than 5-foot-tall, rugged with dark skin enough to suggest he was African. Red-rimmed eyes squinted beneath snow-flecked eyebrows and a floppy red and green hat (yes, we really do wear those things). Ice clumped his beard.

"Is she dead?" he asked.

I nodded. Again, it's something I simply knew: Kathy was as dead as my love for her.

Without me touching it, the chain rattled and unhooked itself. I stepped back, suddenly feeling calm. Peaceful. And free.

I stepped aside to allow the man to enter the room. With both hands he held onto a rope over his shoulder, evidently dragging something on squeaky wheels. A thump and scrape echoed out in the hallway, and I guessed it bounced off a wall, adding another scuff to the council-neglected paintwork.

He wore faded shades of red and green, damp with snow and streaked with what looked like brick dust and flecks of rust. His scuffed boots flicked snow over the thread-bare carpet as he hauled behind him a Christmas parcel as large as a washing machine. It was a colourful box with uneven sides, crooked and dented, with crudely painted snowmen and Big Red – I suspected it had been painted by a child, or someone with absolutely zero artistic talent. The only thing that looked new, or at the very least in good condition, was the beautifully bound ribbon which was bunched up on what was presumably the lid. Such a pristine bow it almost shone in contrast to the dreary décor of our home.

At the time, I of course didn't know it was called a ribbon machine. A device the Elite simply refer to as the Machine. We each have our own, and it's up to us all to keep them in good working order. Our one and only tool of the trade, as it were.

I followed the man into the kitchen.

He released the frayed rope and crouched beside Kathy's lifeless body.

I felt nothing other than intrigue as he poked a finger into my wife's mouth, hooking out a soggy piece of ribbon the same red as the bow. He tucked it into his tunic pocket and stood.

"How are you feeling?" he asked, looking up at me. His eyes were as dark as his skin. Most of the snow had now melted and soaked his clothes, dripping onto the chipped linoleum.

I had no idea what to say.

He smiled with such perfect and very white teeth. "You good with this?"

I nodded.

"The name's Harold." His smile widened. "I know your name. It's good to meet you, Laurence."

Again, I nodded. I felt dumb.

"You're just going through the transition," he explained, "you'll be fine."

And he was correct. I was absolutely fine later, but right then I could only watch him do his thing.

We each have our own speciality. Harold's is choking, as demonstrated first hand to me when I watched my wife die. And I must tell you about another fellow Elite member: Anne, whose speciality is the brain haemorrhage. She was once a neurosurgeon and although a rewarding job when people survived, she'd discovered a pleasure in the moment when people died. Santa's Elite recruited her in no time! Whereas I have a preference for the car crash. I sabotage the brakes on your vehicle by tying a piece of red ribbon somewhere under the bonnet (or *hood*, for you Americans – I cover most of the Western world, by the way). We're all both fast and invisible, so there's no hope in thinking you'd catch us in the act. That red ribbon, used by all of us here in the Elite, does its magic.

So, you understand, we pluck your name from Big Red's Naughty List and then we orchestrate the car crashes, the heart attacks, the classic fall-down-the-stairs-and-subsequent-neck-breaks. Oh, and of course the house fires…

But I'll get to those shortly.

Allow me to tell you that for those like my Kathy,

and the many others on the various levels much, much worse than her, we Elite members put them into our Machines.

When I stood there in the kitchen and watched Harold untie the red bow on that curious box with its crude artwork, I had no idea what to expect. The smell of my failed meal and Kathy's body odour had now been replaced by a heavy, almost metallic odour.

The four sides clattered away. One slid across the linoleum and hit a cupboard door.

At first, I could not make out what the hell I was looking at. It was a peculiar contraption mostly of rusted panels bolted together. Rubber tubes and snaking cables connected various sections and linked a gaping cone at the top of the device. At the rear were three canisters fixed vertically beside one another: two were empty and reflected the kitchen lighting, while the other was filled with a sparkling mix of red and gold.

Very Christmassy, I thought.

Harold winked at me.

"Watch this," he said and lifted Kathy's body with impressive strength given his small stature and her considerable size, literally dead-lifting her overhead only to force her face-first into the cone.

I noted there were bloody smears around the edges.

Immediately the Machine hummed to life. The metal panels rattled as it devoured the body. Kathy's legs wobbled as though uselessly kicking. The floor shook, and the rumbling filled the room. Plates and glasses clinked somewhere in a cupboard, all the while the entire contraption rocked on its wheels.

Harold stepped away and came to stand at my side. From the corner of my eye I saw him look up at me. He was grinning.

The glass canisters began to fill with a purple liquid. By the time Kathy's feet vanished, both canisters were full.

Finally, the Machine quietened.

Harold approached the canisters and pressed a button. Something clicked, and a reel of brilliant red ribbon spun out to coil at his feet. With another prod of the button, the ribbon stopped.

"This will be yours," he told me and picked up the bunched ribbon. "It's traditional."

"What..." I licked my lips. "What do I do with it?"

"It's Big Red's little piece of magic, and you'll use it for a greater cause."

"I will?"

"Sure." He handed it to me.

The ribbon was warm.

And by the time I went for my induction as the newest member of Santa's Elite, that short reel of ribbon didn't last long. In fact, I soon used up both those canisters that were once my useless cheat of a wife.

***

I've been with the Elite for precisely a year, and unfortunately, I'm now up for a disciplinary. Or worse. A very rare case indeed because as long as we successfully continue to reduce the Earth's population growth, we're very much left to our own devices. Or indeed, *with* our own devices.

The thing is, I learned of a colleague who had a penchant for starting fires.

He was behind the tower block disaster, my old home where both my mother and father burned to death. This Elite member, a man named Monty, was usually more careful – before this, he had an excellent record. Instead of using his ribbon to sabotage only his target's 40-a-day habit of cigarette smoking, Monty managed to set fire to the whole apartment… which then became the entire building. As mentioned earlier, 64 people died.

When I found this out, I couldn't help myself and so confronted Monty.

We had a scuffle in the workshop, and what with my car-sabotaging ribbons and his fire-starting ribbons, we managed to start an electrical fire which destroyed the factory where they make presents.

Monty was crushed as the building collapsed (yay!), along with most of the guys in the workshop and adjacent offices (oops).

I suspect my disciplinary is going to be a harsh one and I really do want to keep my job, but at least I know I've done my bit for the planet. I've had an incredibly successful year, and I trust Big Red sees it that way and ultimately lets me off this minor hiccup. Given all my hard work alongside my colleagues in the Elite, I only hope it balances out the devastation here at the North Pole. Sure, the production line for present-building is majorly down – or perhaps temporarily halted – and the fatalities have been huge among our ranks, but the Elite have reduced the

Earth's population by a considerable amount.

That should work in my favour, right?

If it hasn't balanced out, and I really have fucked it up for everyone this year, please accept my apologies.

Hacked

co-written with Patrick R. McDonough

Cade stood beneath the welcoming shelter of the portico and shook rain from his hair. He swiped at the strands that clumped his forehead. Home, finally, after the unreasonable detention Mr Polanski – the affectionately named *Old Polo* – forced on him. No way did he deserve to stay after school, especially given that it was dark and raining.

With a wave of his key card, the door's neon trim flickered red. Unusual. Another wave, this time closer, and it pulsed green. The door clicked open.

He paused over the threshold. Why were the lights out?

"Mom? Dad?"

No answer.

Fully inside, he allowed the door to shut with a clunk that echoed into the darkness. Despite no answer from his parents, it smelled as though dinner was in the oven: mutton, perhaps.

"Lights on," he said.

Nothing.

"*Lights on.*"

Again, no response.

"Smart homes suck balls." He squinted into the gloom and slapped the wall for the manual switch.

Click-click-click. No lights, not even a glow.

"Seriously?"

Farther into the house, his eyes adapting to the near-dark, he hooked off his shoes. One squeaked on the entrance hall floor. The warmth beneath his socks

– albeit a little hotter than usual – took the chill away after that long walk home.

About to head for the kitchen, assuming his parents were there, something in the back room cracked. Or was it a snap? When he stepped out into the hallway, the floor burned. It was hot. He winced, took another step… even hotter. Really? The thermo-regulated flooring had malfunctioned. He leapt along the hallway, footfalls thumping. Once in the back room, his feet froze in contrast to the temperature behind.

"Mom? What's going on?" His voice sounded pathetic and he clenched his teeth. He needed to man-up.

Gunfire blasted overhead.

He ducked and slammed into a side unit. Then farther away, there was a crackle of laughter. Unamused, he knew it hadn't been real gunfire. Tiptoeing across the freezing floor, he reached the back room and nudged open the door. Bookshelves, heaped boxes, and a mound of toys from when he was younger, hid in the shadows. No movement, nor sounds.

Then from the dining room, a voice chattered. Were Mom and Dad playing a trick on him?

He sprinted back over the hot floor panels. More chattering echoed, maybe from the basement. Yeah, that had to be it: Dad was in his workshop messing with him. He was always trying to entertain Cade, but mostly it was annoying and embarrassing.

As he reached the dining room, a light blinked on in the 1950s display cabinet. Just one shelf, spotlighting Mom's collection of porcelain figurines and miniature cars: a tiny drive-in cinema with a four-inch digital screen, which usually played black-and-white creature features on loop. This was something Dad made for a wedding anniversary – always with the lovey-dovey crap, which Cade hated.

It now showed a real-time image of the back of Cade's head. A waddling silhouette walked into the frame from behind, heading straight for him.

A coldness tickled his neck and he spun round.

No one was there.

Facing the display case once again, and... The lights were off.

From behind, down in the basement, something buzzed. He turned, his breath catching as he tried to call for his dad. He coughed, swallowed, and walked toward the open door. At the top of the stairs, he peered into the darkness. Again, there was that buzzing sound.

"Not funny!"

Knowing it was pointless, he flicked the manual light switch. Taking each step slow as they numbed his feet, the familiar smell of paint and grease rose up to him. At the bottom, he squinted into the darkness. He could barely make out the row of retro arcade machines along one wall. Several power lights glowed from his dad's workbench at the end of the room.

A growl crackled nearby.

Cade stiffened.

Every screen flickered, and pixels jittered across each one. Chaotic patterns, multi-coloured at first only to lighten and form crude ovals. Faces, pink blurs, sharpening to become...

"Akito?"

It was the kid Cade supposedly bullied – at least, Old Polo was convinced of such and had therefore given him detention. The images of Akito said nothing, nor did they blink: simply a row of disembodied heads.

"If you're behind all this," Cade said through tight lips, "I'll pound your face in at school tomorrow."

Akito's mouth opened, and a shriek of static blared from every speaker.

Cade yelled and backed up, cupping his ears.

"Stop this!"

Sudden silence.

As one, the screens went blank, plunging the room into darkness again.

His breath rasped.

About to turn and run, a soft light over the workbench came on and made him pause. Cautiously, he approached. On the bench below a wall lined with organized tools, was a power-saw. And... was that blood on the blade?

All he heard now was his rapid breathing.

Beside the power-saw was a bloodied rag. The saw buzzed, rattling on the bench, then stopped. A silence fell on him, almost heavy to the point of wanting to hunch, to shrink into himself. Instead, he yanked the cord from the socket. About to get out of there and leave the madness, he saw something under the rag. He reached for it, hand trembling...

Two fleshy lips slopped out, and several teeth scattered across the floor.

He stumbled back and groaned, tripping over something. His knees smacked the concrete floor.

"Smile!" Akito's voice crackled from the speaker in the toy robot that lay next to him.

"Leave me alone!" He grabbed the thing and hurled it at one of the retro machines. It bounced off a panel and clattered in the shadows.

The screen pixelated and instead of Akito's face, just a pair of lips appeared. No teeth, only lips that curled into a smile.

Cade hurtled for the stairs. He had to get out of there! Lurching up, each step burned his feet. His cry echoed into the darkness as he finally staggered out through the door and into the dining room. The aroma of mutton and peppers wafted from the kitchen.

"Mom? Dad?" He stumbled past the cabinet, not daring to look at the tiny drive-in screen.

Cade knew Akito was a brainiac when it came to computers, so to hack a smart home didn't surprise him... but to also hack arcade machines and toy robots? This was both incredible and a total violation. He certainly never knew the irritating kid was a hacker. And whose were those lips and teeth?

Sickened and dizzy, he tiptoed for the kitchen and heard music. Entering the steamy room, the floor temperature feeling normal, he stopped. Everything was how it should be. The under-cupboard lights glowed, and an unfamiliar rock n' roll tune crackled from somewhere. His dad was at the hob, sitting awkwardly on a stool and leaning over a boiling pot.

"I was calling you," Cade whined. "Why were you ignoring me?"

Something was not right here.

"Dad?"

The man was stiff, almost robotic. The only motion was his arm, and usually he nodded in time with music – he especially loved rock n' roll.

Cade went to reach for his dad's shoulder, but instead whimpered.

Where the man's lips and front teeth should have been was now a raw mess of jagged flesh and dark blood. Crammed into his swollen mouth was the speaker. Like a toothpick, a small antenna protruded from between the remaining teeth: a remote receiver. Beneath fluttering lashes, his eyes rolled and showed mostly their whites.

"Dad…" Cade tasted bile rise to the back of his throat.

With the same gaffer-tape that fixed the man to the stool, his hand was fastened to a wooden spoon. His arm whirred and clicked beneath metal rods and clunky mechanisms, round and round, stirring whatever it was that boiled.

And still the rock n' roll played.

Inhaling the aroma of meat, Cade saw what looked like sausage churning in the pink water.

Whirring and clicking, round and round…

Not sausage. It was a pale and bloated finger wearing a wedding ring.

"Mom!"

He staggered away as the oven alarm buzzed.

Someone walked in from the pantry.

"Akito!" The buzzing noise filled Cade's head.

The kid wiped glistening hands down the already-bloodied apron he wore – Cade recognised it: his mom's.

"Earlier you stole my sandwich and spat it back at

me," Akito said over the warbling alarm, "so I guess you prefer your meat rare."

"You…"

"If I've overcooked her, there's plenty left in the freezer."

The Incident at Trent Home

To ask Gran for help with a school project was a first for Jack, his initial reluctance shrugged off by Mum who'd suggested it. Fifteen years old, pimpled and awkward, and quietly intelligent, Jack would have never suspected he'd end up in hospital, wrapped in bandages while questioned by police. None of what happened was, he told the investigators, his fault.

Jack Dempsey left out nothing in his retelling of the incident at Trent Home.

Last day of term and with his school bag slung over a skinny shoulder, he'd made his way along the corridor to Gran's apartment, thankful to be indoors away from the relentless autumn wind. Flanked by magnolia walls beneath dim lighting, his footsteps echoed off the chipped and stained floor tiles. The subtle odour of damp mixed with a heavy reek of meaty dinner strengthened the deeper into the 'old people's home' he went – Mum didn't like it when he used that phrase. The Home wasn't strictly a care home, it was more a not-too-expensive place for stubborn octogenarians and nonagenarians who refused to go into a proper home.

Jack knew writing an essay about the Second World War would be much easier if he used the school library. Of course he could trawl the internet like most of his classmates, but Gran, as Mum insisted, had first-hand experience as a child living in Britain strangled by the fear of invasion.

Jack rounded the corner into the final corridor towards Gran's apartment and saw her door ajar.

Unusual, he thought as he eyed a subtle flickering light – the TV, he assumed – that sent a white haze across the frame and along the wall. He slowed his approach and lifted a hand ready to push the door.

"Gran?" His voice fell into the silence.

No answer.

He nudged the door and it swung inwards. A stickiness remained on his fingertips, and he rubbed it away. The stuff crumbled to a chalky powder. His lip curled and he stepped inside. The stink of overcooked dinner snatched his breath and he coughed. Across the room, the TV, a bulky relic among other dated furniture, was a rectangle of silent white static. Its glare accentuated by the approach of sunset that pressed against closed curtains.

"Gran?"

As before, there was no answer.

The heat was unbearable, which made him wonder if the thermostat was cranked too high. After dropping his bag in the corner of the room, he frantically removed his coat and draped it over the back of a chair.

"Gran!"

He headed across the lounge and into the kitchen. No Gran. Then back into the lounge and to the bedroom. No Gran. A quick peek under the bed revealed nothing – not that he'd expected her to actually be under there. The bathroom proved equally empty. Where was she? The front door had been open, after all, so perhaps she was out visiting a neighbour or got caught chatting with the warden (Gran was always trying to influence the running of the Home somehow). *Perhaps*, he thought, *she'd forgotten today's visit.*

About to head for the sofa to sit and wait her return, he heard something shuffle on the other side of the room. He squinted into clustered shadows beneath a small table and armchair. Pets weren't allowed in the Home, so he knew it wasn't an animal – at least it shouldn't be.

Jack stepped forward, curious.

Something pale shifted in the layers of darkness, but it was difficult to tell. And again, there was that sound.

Then silence. No movement.

He crouched, his own shadow dancing up the wall, and he peered behind the armchair.

Beside a modest drinks cabinet and coiled TV cables, was a hole in the wall. The plaster looked as though someone had booted it in. Amid splintered skirting and torn wallpaper, a light dust covered the carpet – not dissimilar to pastry flakes. Inside the cavity revealed only darkness.

Listening intently, he heard nothing.

The meaty odour was stronger, mingled with a wet earthiness.

Slowly he straightened, dismissing it as noises from the neighbour or maybe even his imagination. Then from inside the wall, higher up, something slumped. A coldness spread up the back of his neck, defying the room's heat. He eyed the wall, expecting… expecting *what* precisely?

Slowly, he started to back up.

The wall bulged, cracked and—

Jack had no idea what the grey thing was as it burst through the wall. Blinded by chunks of plaster and curls of wallpaper, whatever it was slammed into him. His breath rushed from his lungs. He staggered back. Tripped on the rug. And went down, backwards. His head smacked the table.

The flickering light switched to a warm and welcoming darkness.

***

When Jack came to, he found he wasn't on the rug. Instead, he sat upright amid the contents of his school bag. Folders and papers strewn about him. Pens and pencils scattered in between. And a thin layer of that sticky substance coated everything. Not to mention brick dust and sheets of torn wallpaper.

His head thumped and there was a subtle roaring in his ears.

How…? What…? He pushed himself up onto his knees though a dizziness prevented him from standing. Through his bewilderment he watched a cloud of dust drift away from his clothes. It was spotlighted by the setting sun's final rays through a gap in the curtains. The flickering TV set was now the room's only illumination. How long had he been unconscious?

He dragged a hand down his face and winced. His fingers came away bloody.

The collapsed section of wall filled part of the room and when he peered into the gaping cavity, he remembered something. His heart leapt into his throat. The grey *thing* that had broken through was nowhere to be seen. Maybe… maybe he'd imagined it. The wall had evidently collapsed, due to damp perhaps, and knocked him unconscious. There was nothing lurking inside the wall. He was being ridiculous.

Again, this time cautiously, he touched the wound at his temple.

The silence of Gran's apartment seemed somehow thicker, and that strange meaty smell was heavier. Where was Gran? He stood, ready to get out of there; he had to call the warden, and call Mum.

Rather than over the back of the chair where he'd left it, his coat was now on the floor against his upended school bag. As fast as his shaky legs allowed, he went over to it and saw how that too was covered in more of the peculiar gunk. He rummaged in the pockets for his phone.

It wasn't there.

He turned, confusion and his pounding headache threatening to bring him to his knees.

His phone was beside the skirting board, its screen a mass of cracks beneath a smearing of that glistening filth. He scrambled over to it and, although the screen lit up behind the shattered web of glass, found it unresponsive to any finger tap. He dropped it, stood up and wiped the sticky mess from his fingertips, and went for Gran's telephone. More of the peculiar shit coated that, too. Trying not to freak out, he snatched up the receiver, disgusted at the grittiness. There was only silence. This didn't surprise him. Angrily, he jabbed the buttons though this failed to bring a dial tone.

His heartbeat now filled his head, pulsing as rapidly as his breathing. Perhaps Gran was downstairs in the common room. If not, maybe a neighbour could help. With one final glance around the room and a reluctant scan of the ruined wall, he stepped out into the corridor. Lifting a hand to shield his eyes from the overhead lights, his knuckles brushed his head wound and he hissed through clenched teeth.

Every footfall sent shockwaves into his skull as he made his way along the corridor towards the stairwell.

Just before the landing was a highbacked armchair – a common spot for a resident to sit and gaze out the window. Jack almost didn't spot the gentleman sitting there, such was the man's small stature and the way he had his legs curled up beneath him on the cushion. It looked incredibly uncomfortable. The darkening sky beyond the window gave way to his gaunt reflection, creating a pale image. Jack recognised him though didn't know his name. He was dressed in a worn brown suit, collar open to reveal wrinkled skin and curls of white hair. His head was tilted back, mouth slightly parted. Asleep. Hopefully.

Jack's pace slowed, though he stopped when he saw the blood at the man's temples.

But it wasn't just blood. Mottled folds of a strange dough-like substance had spread up the chair from a hole in the wall. It clamped the side of the man's head, digging its way beneath the puckered skin. A glistening fluid oozed from the wound, trickling down his face to mingle with his blood.

A sickness churned in Jack's stomach. He reached up to his own temple, wincing as his fingers probed the wound. A giddiness stole him and he reached out.

His fingers slid across the wall, leaving bloody trails. His lungs suddenly tightened. Looking down at the floor, desperate to compose himself, he spotted how the floor tiles had been forced upwards near the man's feet, revealing a bulging doughy trunk. It splayed outwards like grasping seaweed shrivelled in the sun.

The man's eyelids flickered. The wound dribbled. He groaned, spit bubbling at his lips.

Jack straightened up, staggered, and darted past him. He rounded the corner and onto the stairwell landing. Taking the stairs two at a time, he almost fell, frantically clawing at his head, grimacing against the pain as he tried to wipe away the blood, the infection, whatever that disgusting stuff was.

Finally downstairs, into another corridor identical to upstairs, he spotted more of those cracks. He noticed other apartment doors were open, each filled with failing daylight, but he ignored them. He hoped Gran was okay, sitting in her favourite chair in the common room, playing cards or Scrabble with friends, completely safe.

Almost there now, although in truth he wanted nothing more than to get the hell out of Trent Home.

Avoiding more holes in the walls, he spotted an even thicker fold of doughy whatever-it-was hanging overhead. It had broken through one wall, crept across the ceiling and forced its way into the opposite wall. The undulating trunk, slick with moisture, was darker down here compared with the one he'd seen upstairs. And longer. The path of which emerged from the common room wall.

He slowed, fearing the worst, fighting the urge to

turn and run and—

Voices.

Soft conversation.

All was normal. Please.

He calmed his breath and placed a trembling hand on the door. That familiar grittiness covered the wooden panel. He pushed the door to be greeted with a heat and stink that forced itself down his throat.

***

Jack's legs failed him and he tried to grab the door handle, missed, and fell over the threshold. On his knees, desperate to get his feet beneath him, he stared into the gloom of the common room.

What appeared to be most of Trent Home's residents were here, several dozen at a guess, yet it was impossible to count. Although everyone was *kind of* sprawled across the floor, some piled atop one another, each fused with the next like melted candle wax.

The voices came from mouths where there shouldn't have been mouths.

Pushed up against three corners of the room amid upended chairs, the residents combined were a fleshy sprawl of torn clothing and skin and bone. Their mottled and liver-spotted skin stretched taut to become shivering membranes. In places, arm and leg bones protruded at wrong angles, skulls and ribcages jutted through glistening organs. Blood dribbled from gashes.

Not only was it the mouths in the wrong places, it was also every nose, every eye, every ear. Other body parts, too. Armpits and elbows, droopy breasts, grey pubic mounds, and wrinkled buttocks. Everything defied human anatomy.

Repulsed, Jack blinked away tears. He wiped at his face, conscious of how his head throbbed. He didn't know where to look.

And that was just it: Looking... It was as though every resident somehow *looked* back at him. Their eyes were not dead stares as he would have suspected. Some were lidless, others sunken in fleshy folds, but all had floating gazes, focusing on nothing. Yet he felt as though everyone stared at him.

Vomit burned up his throat and he gulped it down.

Conduits of flesh had reached out across the carpet, coiled between broken chair legs and scattered cushions, clung to the walls like giant fingers. Picture frames hung askew, the glass cracked. Lengths of quivering membrane stretched from one corner of the room to another like pink and veiny sails, attached to light fittings, table surfaces, and windowsills. The stretched flesh was occasionally broken by the throbbing muscle of an exposed heart, or the rhythmic rise and fall of lungs, or the shake of deformed legs and arms. Even the occasional flick of an arthritic finger and twitch of a shrivelled penis. Several black and white photographs were clutched in a number of gnarly knuckles.

And those mouths. Those wet lips, those flicking tongues and chattering teeth, forming words, sentences. Every mouth in the room spoke at once. An insane cacophony, like a heated debate where all those present demanded attention.

"…clatter of machine gun fire…"

"…held his hand as he died…"

"…last time I saw my father…"

"…evil time where many died…"

"…never saw my brother again…"

"…roar overhead as a Spitfire chased a Messerschmitt…"

Jack hugged himself, unable to tear his eyes from the heaped monstrosity that filled the room. He weakly clutched at his head, willing the pain at his temple to calm.

The nearest sweaty sack of flesh shivered and ballooned. Its floral dress tore as an arm – or was it a spindly leg? – reached out to him. Faint blue veins wriggled beneath translucent flesh, the bones beneath impossibly thin. Flat, almost.

Jack recoiled and the door jamb whacked his spine. He turned to stand up on legs that failed to obey.

"Gran," he whispered.

It was the dress he recognised rather than her face. Because it wasn't her face any longer. Her frizzy hair still clung to a skull that had fused with the warped skeleton of someone else. Gran's chair – her favourite chair – had collapsed beneath the weight while apparently absorbing another resident's body. The two women were now one huge, bloated mound of flesh and bone, stitched together in a mass of wrinkled skin dotted with liver spots. Her eyes had dropped somewhere down her lengthened cheeks, eyelids droopy, her chin now a part of her spine that had twisted and now jutted awkwardly. Her spectacles had sunken into her clavicle, buried in a veiny membrane that blended with elongated breasts. Their bristly areolas were wrinkled ovals sporting nipples that resembled sultanas.

Jack scrambled sidewards, farther into the room, kicking away from her.

"My friends have helped us," she said through lips wet with dribble.

"Get off me!" he shrieked.

He scrambled upwards, clutching feebly at the wall. He slipped and fell against the rise of flesh as the thing that was his gran tried to hold him. He sprawled against her. This wasn't Gran, this couldn't be. This was impossible.

The smell was a mix of lavender and sweaty skin. Cloying, it sent waves of nausea to flood through him. He gasped for air, only to succeed in filling his lungs with the stink. He coughed and choked. Saggy folds slapped around him like wet leather. A damp stickiness slopped down his cheek. Unable to escape her, he sank into the slippery embrace. He shoved himself away, scrambling backwards, pushing against her greyish, prickly areolas. Searing pain fired through his head as tiny pseudopods snaked into the wound at his temple. He screamed, long and loud.

"You will get top grades, Jack," she whispered, though he couldn't hear her.

His screams lasted longer than the heartbeat of every resident of Trent Home. Including Gran, whose eyes were the endmost to glaze over. Eventually, still cradled in those clammy folds of skin, his sobs took him into a peaceful oblivion.

Hours later in hospital, with a bandaged head and

Mum at his bedside, Jack's mind was heavy with memories that were not his own.

Gran had indeed helped him with his school project.

The Thing Inside

Barely 12 years old, and in as many minutes I had witnessed enough death to last a lifetime. Impossible for me to know that as I stumbled up the beach and away from the crashing waves, there would be much more death throughout the many years to follow.

Through the fog, I spotted a jagged silhouette. More derelict than humble, perhaps a hundred feet ahead, the building was a hazy refuge I had to reach.

Shivers wracked my frail body, and every footfall sent hammer blows to my skull. An odd combination of copper and salt filled my mouth, and each gasp sucked cold air into my lungs. My tunic and trousers were soaked rags clinging to lacerated skin. Everywhere ached, and my weakening knees threatened to take me down into blackness.

To survive the sinking ship was a feat I would soon ponder, though with cold shingle beneath bare feet I had but one thought: to get as far from the sea as my stumbling allowed. The roar of waves, the flapping and tearing of sails, the snap of splintered timber, all echoed in my head. Such a furious and haunting cacophony, mingled with the remembered cries of drowning fellow passengers and crew.

I hugged myself with blood-slick fingers and clamped my jaw closed to stop my teeth chattering.

Shingle became pebbles that clacked and crunched, and each step brought me closer to collapse. Several times I wanted to sit, to close my eyes and await death that I somehow knew would never come.

The moonlight gave the fog a milkiness which

crawled across the pebbles like a deflated cloud. One foot ... in front ... of the other. At an ever-decreasing pace, across the levelling beach, I neared and eventually reached the threshold of my chosen shelter.

Its timber walls were crooked and warped with a half-collapsed chimney stack of pitted brickwork. The entrance gaped where tangled fishing nets bulged as though vomited. What was once a tiled roof was little more than crossed rafters wrapped in brambles.

I clutched the rotten doorframe. My fingers sank into soft splinters – firm enough, however, to keep me upright.

The place reeked of wet vegetation and rancid fish. Fog-shrouded moonlight pressed in through the rafters to highlight the mildewed walls, tufts of determined grass, and buckled floorboards. My vision shifted in and out of focus. The wind whistled through gaps in the planks, creating an occasional crack and snap on loose fixings.

I stumbled over the fishing nets, and the boards creaked. My movements dragged and it felt like I still struggled beneath the waves, gulping for air. Finally, away from the wind and dank fog, I dropped to my already bruised and bloody knees.

A strange silence engulfed me and accentuated the volume of my harsh breathing. I snatched at the net, pulled it around me as though it were a blanket, and curled into it.

That's when I saw the woman.

Apparently oblivious to my entrance, she crouched by a gaping hole in the far wall. Crooked planks framed her small stature making her appear only as a silhouette against roiling fog. Hair obscured her face where she hunched over, shifting floorboards back into place. They knocked and banged together.

She said something, words little more than a whisper, though I could not make them out, such was the blood rushing through my head, the relentless wind … and echoes from the catastrophe I had left behind.

The woman threw a furtive glance over a shoulder, out through the section of broken wall. Hurriedly she stood and again peered outside, this time looking to the left and then to the right. Satisfied, I assumed, that no one saw her, she took exit, leaving me with a blurred view as she vanished into the fog. For a moment, the mist thinned and there, not too far away, was a yellow glow. Square, a welcoming light, a beacon only for her. A window, perhaps.

A sharp pain at the back of my neck sent lightning into my brain.

I cried out and curled even tighter into the pathetic embrace of net. Touching my neck just above the hairline, my finger slid into a deep wound. Slick, hot. Unbearable pain swept over me. I quickly withdrew my hand. Another stab of agony shot through my skull …

Unconsciousness stole me away. But not before I glimpsed a fisherman's cottage that squatted farther up the beach.

***

When I came to in the man's thick arms, a woman's voice drifted towards me. It seemed to float on the aroma of tobacco and meaty stew. I had no idea where I was or how I got there, and for a moment I suspected I was still on the sinking ship. But no. The voice – more a *shriek* – came from the woman who stood before a stove. She wore a crimson shawl, ragged, and scarred with holes. Her knuckles were bony and white from where she clutched it beneath her chin.

She peered at me with tiny eyes.

"Have you forgotten about *our* boy?" she said through tight lips.

The man took me fully into their home, into a warmth more from steam rather than the dying embers in the hearth. He placed me down on a small, hard bed in the corner of the squalid room.

"We can't leave him out there," he said. "Look at the state of the poor thing."

"We know nothing about him. We cannot have him in our home."

"It's our Christian duty."

"Who is he?" she demanded. The way she hunched over the stove was familiar: the woman from the abandoned hut.

"He said his name is Sydney. I don't know where he's from."

"We cannot have him here."

"He needs our help." The man stepped back from the bed. A cloud of tobacco formed around his hat. It was the type every fisherman wore. "He muttered something about a *Josephine Willis* and that it sank. I suspect that was the ship he was on."

It hurt to even nod, to even acknowledge the truth behind the man's words. I could not remember telling him about the packet ship, *Josephine Willis*, upon which I was a passenger. Had I told him how it left London to head for New Zealand? About my parents on board, too? Had I told him how the great steel steamer tore through the hull of the *Josephine*? And what of the crew and passengers drowning, leaving only me to survive?

"I do not care." Stepping away from the stove, the woman snatched up a cloth. Her knuckles whitened and she twisted it. "This is a dishonour to our William!"

The man puffed on his pipe, and slowly said, "William is dead. Gone."

"Don't say that!" She turned from him.

"It's been two months."

"I don't want to hear it!"

"I have to go back out." He gestured to me. "Clean him up, Nancy. I want you to dress his wounds, feed him. Give him my plate."

"What?"

"Do it. I'm not hungry."

"But—"

"Nancy, look after the boy. It was a miracle I found him."

The flickering candlelight, the moist heat, the smell of cooking, all swamped me. It came at me in waves like I was again drowning. The room suffocated me, pressing in on my vision.

Nancy's voice sounded far away as she replied: "We *had* a miracle once …"

I floated in and out of consciousness for however long it took the woman to tend my wounds. Without any gentleness, she scrubbed my cuts and grazes and pulled me around at all angles. The pain was numbed by dizziness and confusion, and I would be shushed if I groaned or called out. When it came to her treating the lacerations on my chest, she showed no compassion. It was as though to her I was just another chore. She paid no attention to the wound in my hairline at the base of my skull. Eventually she left me alone.

Feeling somewhat constricted by the tight bandages, I stared up at the cobwebbed rafters of a low ceiling. My entire body ached with the occasional painful reminder of the wound at the back of my head. I somehow fell into a restless and far from fitful sleep.

Days passed and the man, whose name I learned was George, kept checking on me. He'd sit by my side at all hours between what I assumed were his fishing duties, smelling of a strange mix of tobacco, sweat, and fish. All the while Nancy would ignore me. The only attention she would give me was when George told her to set me a plate of food or see to my bandages.

Always, always with reluctance.

Within days the number of bandages which covered me decreased, and on one occasion I witnessed a strange look in Nancy's eyes. It was more than reluctance this time, much more than annoyance or indeed the utter displeasure of having me in her home; the look she gave me was surprise. She hastily, if a little lazily, wrapped me up. When I huddled beneath the blanket, I perhaps even caught her looking at me with suspicion.

It wasn't until later that day while I drifted in and out of a doze, I overheard her speak with George.

"… unnatural," she was saying. "Those wounds have healed incredibly swiftly."

"He's a strong lad."

There was pride in his voice and for that I listened intently, purposefully not moving to feign sleep.

"Those deep cuts in his chest," Nancy added, "are all but closed up now."

"Strong, as I say."

The floorboards creaked, and I sensed he was close to my bed. Still, I pretended to sleep.

Nancy's whisper: "The Devil's work, I suspect."

"I'll hear nothing of the sort." George's voice was far from a whisper. "That is ridiculous."

I groaned and turned, still keeping my eyes closed. I had no desire to hear more arguments. Since my arrival at their home in Dungeness their exchanges were often tense, undoubtedly caused in part by the sad death of their son; if they were not arguing over my being there, they bickered over mundane things. Not once did I witness the love I remember my own parents shared.

When I thought of my mother and father beneath the waves, lost to me forever, I bit my lip and sobbed into my own personal darkness. I could not imagine Nancy's response should she ever see my tears.

Another couple of days passed and I eventually wore only one bandage beneath a loose tunic I assumed belonged to George. The occasional sharp pain from neck to brain continued, all-too-familiar now, but was no longer severe. My recovery, my healing, was undeniably rapid, and I felt stronger and strangely more alert – this last, I put down to settling into a new environment.

Yet something told me to reign it in, and not dare reveal how I felt. Somehow, I knew I had to play it out. If only for a while longer.

***

"I have something for you," George said.

From the stove, Nancy's eyes narrowed and she looked across at her husband.

His face wrinkled into that wide grin I had warmed to. He held something just out of sight, awkwardly to his side, and sat on the edge of my mattress that had long-since become chair, table, and a place to rest. Not once had I been allowed to join them at dinner times around their crooked table. Indeed, I rarely even ate with them and my bowl would always be filled with what amounted to leftovers.

A week since my arrival, and my chest remained bandaged. Yet without having inspected them, I knew the wounds beneath were now entirely healed. This was something I did not want to reveal, not even to George. The back of my neck still hurt, however, and sometimes it would pulse, tingling up and down my spine.

I shuffled closer to the man. He smelled of that familiar combination of fish, sweat, and tobacco.

"A gift." His lips twitched around his pipe. "Something I made."

For a moment he glanced away and then he winked at me, holding out a piece of driftwood. It was carved into the shape of a ship's hull complete with white fabric in way of a sail, stitched with string around a slightly crooked mast.

I smiled. Perhaps the first genuine smile in a long time.

He handed the ship to me. It was much lighter than it looked. With one hand cupping the smooth hull, I ran a finger down the mast which was once a thin branch, now with its bark removed.

"Do you like it?"

Tears pricked my eyes.

He laughed. "I'll take that as a yes, little man."

My mouth had gone dry and I tried to say *thank you*. With an even louder laugh, he ruffled my hair.

Floorboards creaked from somewhere close by, but I ignored the sound. Regardless of everything endured on the *Josephine*, the loss of my parents, my survival in the sea, the restless nights while healing, in that moment as I clutched the driftwood ship I knew everything would be okay. I would recover from my injuries, physically and mentally. This man here was going to care for me, and despite Nancy's hostility I had no doubt she would eventually soften. When I saw much love in this man's eyes, she too would love me with equal measure.

Pressing that wooden ship close to my heart was all the evidence I needed. Finally, I trusted all would be fine. I had a future.

And then the ship flew from my hands.

It bounced into the middle of the room. The mast remained attached by only a single thread. My empty hands stung.

Nancy's shriek filled the cottage: "What do you think you're doing?"

"Nancy!" George clenched his pipe between yellow teeth. He stood. "I made—"

"Did you ever make anything for William?"

"What are you—?"

"You didn't once make our son a wooden … ship!"

"I never had a chance, he—"

"Don't say it. Don't you dare!"

She pulled away when he tried to grasp her shoulder.

He said, "By the time William would've been old enough to play with something—"

"Shut up!"

"—like that, he was too weak. He was only four years old."

"You never made him anything!"

"I loved him as much as you."

"I still love him."

"As do I, Nancy."

"You want to replace William with *him*." She pointed to me.

Her finger seemed as long as the snapped mast of the driftwood ship. Her broken fingernail glistened in the firelight. Vegetable juice smeared her knuckles.

"I do not want to replace our son." George had both hands on his hips. "But we have been given another chance."

"I never wanted another chance!" She wiped away her tears.

"Sydney here is a gift from God."

"Do not bring the Lord into this. He chose to take away our son. I am done with Him!"

George again reached for her, and again she recoiled.

"Nancy, please. We are here to take this boy in as our own."

"No! No, we are not!"

"We've been over this—"

She pushed her way past him. Her shawl slipped from her shoulders and fell silently to the floor. She bent down to grab the broken ship ... and hurled it towards the fire. The sail flapped like a broken wing.

Flames claimed it.

I scrambled from the bed, reaching out.

George shouted, "Don't!"

He grabbed me, held me firm, and I watched the flames leap around the hull. The sail flared, shrivelled. Smoke billowed.

"Get off!"

While I squirmed, from the corner of my eye I saw Nancy run out the house. Cold air replaced her from where the door swung back in the frame. I twisted in George's arms and managed to free myself.

"Sydney!"

I reached into the fire.

"Stop!"

The flames engulfed my hands, and instead of pain there was a heat at the back of my neck. It flared outwards from the now-healed wound.

"What are you doing?" George yanked me back.

A disconnected pain ebbed with the heat from my neck as I clutched the blackened driftwood. I slapped at the remaining flames leaving only smoke to curl along the wood grains.

"Foolish boy!"

My palms were streaked black. No pain. In the fireplace, the mast burned fiercely atop ash that had once been the sail. Tears came. I cried at the loss of my parents. I cried for George's ruined gift. I cried because Nancy would never love me. I cried for this man who held me. And I cried in recognising the significance of the changes I sensed within me. Beyond any natural healing, something gained strength.

***

Nancy took it upon herself to ignore me for over a week. During which time, and on a number of mornings, I awoke to discover peculiar dirt on my feet: sticky, tar-like. Who was to say I hadn't spent the nights walking outside in my sleep? I had of course bathed since my recovery – at least when Nancy allowed me to use a small pan of cold water – but this was puzzling. I thought little of it, rather more curious as to my strengthening knowledge that I harboured something beyond my mere 12-year-old body, something which had allowed me to survive drowning, to heal swiftly, and to separate a pain that otherwise should burn.

The blackened driftwood, the remains of George's magnificent handcrafted gift, was kept safely underneath my bed. When Nancy was away from the cottage, I would often remove it to simply look at. A constant reminder of two things: George's love for me, and a growing strength within.

No longer wrapped in any bandage, if I wasn't sitting on the front step of the cottage awaiting George's return from a day's haul I would run across the beach. There was a lighthouse much farther along the shingle where I sometimes questioned how it failed in its duty and allowed the sea to swallow the *Josephine Willis*. I avoided the other fishing cottages, never wanting the attention of another adult and certainly to ignore the few children there. When I first encountered the other younger occupants of Dungeness, I deliberately turned deaf to their taunts. I was beyond them; of that I had no doubt. On occasion I spent time outside with George, where he would teach me simple fishing tasks or what he was about when out to sea. He often said I would one day accompany him, to be at his side during the greatest haul of his life. He said it with such conviction, with immense pride, that I believed him.

At least, I wanted to believe him; deep down that ever-growing presence within told me otherwise …

When Nancy eventually spoke to me, it was when a storm kept George out to sea. The way she repeatedly opened the front door to look outside was the only time I saw anything that could be seen as love towards her husband.

The wind howled outside, thunder and lightning raging beyond the cottage walls. I lay on my bed watching cobwebs quiver in the rafters, their shadows dancing across the ceiling. Another crack of lightning lit up the sky through the hazy window, and I glanced at Nancy. She sat at the table, hunched. Her reflection flashed in the glass like a pale ghost, beside which the oil lantern burned bright.

"When will he be home?" I asked.

She didn't answer, didn't even look at me. Something I was used to by now.

"I hope he's okay," I added. "Please, when will George get home?"

"What do you care?" Her voice was barely above a whisper.

"Of course I care." It pained me to hear her say such a thing. I wanted to get out of there, despite the horrid weather.

She stood. "No, you don't care."

"I—"

"You're not family." She turned from the window and was beside my bed in an instant. Her eyes mirrored the fire that crackled in the hearth.

My heartbeat raced, my breath coming in short gasps.

Her hand swung up and slapped my cheek.

Its sharpness stung and a rising heat spread to my head. I glared at her, clenching my teeth. My hands became fists and that heat continued to surge through my arms and legs.

But … somehow … I stayed where I was. Something inside me prevented me from retaliating, indeed something *told* me to bide my time.

She turned on her heel and stomped to the window as another roar of thunder shook the walls.

Despite the raging storm, the silence between us thickened.

I remained awake until well past midnight, tormented by thoughts of never again seeing George while the thunder and lightning soon gave way to relentless wind and rain. The last thing I saw before an exhausted sleep finally came was how Nancy kept vigil at the window, squinting into the darkness beyond the cottage.

***

My sleep was restless, filled with haunting voices from the sea and echoes of the drowned, and that reassuring presence within, growing, waiting, and revealing how it became a part of me. When I awoke, however, I was left with fleeting images, snatches of truth from the moment seawater filled my lungs, starved me of oxygen, and killed me; the moment I had died only to return to life by becoming host to some*thing*.

As a weak sunrise pushed light through the windows, I remained in bed and watched Nancy leave the cottage. Her despondent glance, mixed with a familiar hatred, strengthened the determination to learn of what was inside me, to seek the truth through my dreams, my nightmares.

I wanted to join Nancy in searching for George, yet instead I remained indoors searching within myself.

There had been a cargo crate, one of many, with splintered boards and frayed rope that moved in the water like eels. There were crashing waves creating powerful currents to steal me into the depths. Beneath the waves, tumbling with my flailing limbs, pottery and crockery drifted, wrapped in clumps of straw packaging. And there was something dark, as large as a barrel. Perhaps a great stone or rock, something with too many irregular edges and angles, sleek with traces of glowing amber. Yet was it a reflection of flames from the sinking ship?

The more I thought of it, the more the images evaded me, floated away, left to tease, and suggest nothing more than simply troubled dreams.

During the latter part of the morning when the only evidence of the previous night's storm was tangled seaweed and driftwood washed up along the beach, George returned.

Nancy had been gone for hours, and I sat on the front step watching a gentle wind sway the grass tufts which sprouted between pebbles. All the while hoping for George's safety, I was still trying to recall my dreams.

When George and Nancy walked towards the cottage, it was as though I felt the tension drain from me. I ran to him, almost tripping in the grass that only moments before I found mesmerising and wrapped my arms around his waist. His clothes were drenched. He didn't wear his hat, yet still his pipe jutted from tight lips. He ruffled my hair, but the gesture was void of its usual enthusiasm. As we stood together in an embrace I wanted to last forever, Nancy, I noted, continued walking towards the cottage. She kept glancing over to the abandoned hut. For a moment it seemed she hesitated, wanting to go there rather than home. I hugged George tightly and still watched Nancy, wishing for her to come back with us rather than visit that place. Still clinging to George, sensing his eagerness to return indoors, I was clueless as to why I felt relieved to see she continued to head for the cottage. I finally released him, and we walked, my small hand in his loose and calloused grip.

With Nancy leading the way, she came to wait for us on the front step. George's tiredness was evident in both the way he chewed his unlit pipe and how he dragged every step.

Finally inside, I closed the door behind us. Already unbuttoning his clothes, George disappeared into their bedroom while Nancy went over to the stove. She threw me a look that said: *don't you dare tell him I laid a hand upon you.*

***

With George sleeping and Nancy busying herself around the cottage, I spent the afternoon on the beach collecting debris left by the storm. Come twilight, as a murky haze settled over the Dungeness peninsular, I had created what to me was a mountain of driftwood and broken fishing crates, tangled with fishing nets and seaweed. It was an entirely pointless task, however it succeeded in banishing thoughts of my dreams. It was as though, in the light of day, I chastised myself for that need to learn what it was that truly happened to me when the *Josephine Willis* sank. Yet, as the sky darkened and pressed down on my tired shoulders, I again began to scrutinise those lingering fragments of dream.

Lying back on one of the final rises of pebbles before it dropped down to the sea, fatigue soon took me into an early-evening doze. I expected any time soon to hear George call me in for supper, assuming he'd be up and about by then (he had appeared to have no injuries from the storm, regardless of the battered state of his boat, and needed sleep. As did I).

I jolted awake, the darkness of night now upon me, along with a heavy odour of seaweed. Without any lingering image of dream – or nightmare – the cold glow of moonlight behind fast moving clouds illuminated my surroundings. I gulped the salty wind coming off the sea, and for a moment wondered where I was. I shivered, and huddled up against a damp beam of driftwood as thick as my leg.

Sitting up, I felt a stickiness and gloopy mess covering my hands and forearms. Given the silvery gloom, it appeared as though I had dipped my arms in tar: the same residue discovered when awakening on previous mornings. I rubbed my fingers together, noticing its grittiness. In a poor attempt to rid myself of the filth, I wiped my hands through the grassy tufts either side of me.

I paused, confused. Earlier when I had dozed, I was not anywhere near vegetation. What was going on? I jerked upright, even straighter, glaring about me.

No longer near the sea, nowhere near where I had been earlier, I was now between the cottage and the abandoned hut.

I stood, hugging myself – a useless attempt for comfort. The only comfort, unsurprisingly, was the warmth at the base of my skull. Soothing, reassuring. Confidence washed over me, and I started to walk towards the cottage. I had to clean myself up. Immediately. My shoes squelched with each footfall: they were covered in that black tar-like matter.

While I walked, I glanced at the derelict hut.

Something at the corner of my eye had moved. Perhaps it was only the mist, such were the thick shadows collected around the crooked structure, especially inside the collapsed section of wall.

Before going indoors, certain to avoid passing any window to not bring myself to Nancy's attention, I headed round the back of the cottage. I crouched beside a bucket I knew George often used for cleaning. In the near-darkness, I scrubbed with oily rags with such frantic actions I heard only my panicky breath. I eyed the nearest window. It was the bedroom. There would be no reason for anyone, least of all Nancy, to be there. About to stand, I convinced myself I saw something red move inside the room. Nancy's crimson shawl?

I shook off the thought and headed inside.

With George still sleeping, Nancy had taken it upon herself to fail to call me in for supper. She did not even acknowledge my return. This silence, as I headed for bed, reinforced my acceptance that she did not care what I had been doing or where I had been.

***

Just before sunrise, I again woke with that overpowering earthy smell, and as I swung my legs out of bed, I saw my toes caked with filth. It covered my blanket, too.

Before anyone else woke, I made certain to be out of the cottage as quiet as possible, and headed for the bucket of water I had used the previous night. I had to clean up before anyone saw, especially Nancy.

The cold water was enough to bring me fully awake as I used the already-filthy rag that reeked of oil and fish and was slick with the peculiar matter. In the pale blue gloom of dawn, before the sun properly rose, I inspected the substance that I scrubbed away. In the dark of night, I had likened it to tar, but now I saw clumps of reds and yellows. Similar to sand, albeit stringy like a fungus, and brittle. Crumbling in places, it was certainly vegetative in nature, and much thicker and sinewy than on previous occasions.

Before heading back indoors, I walked around the cottage with the unshakeable desire to see the derelict hut from afar. I had no doubt that it was there I had been visiting, evidently while I slept. But why? And how did I know this?

Seeing the mist drift across from the sea, the collapsed structure reminded me of when I'd first arrived there in Dungeness. From that distance, perhaps I saw a silhouette, a ghostly spectre lurking in the shadows of the collapsed wall. Nancy? Again, I was reminded of having survived the sinking of the *Josephine*, taking refuge in the hut, and seeing her there. Yet now, such was the blue-grey light of approaching sunrise, the more I squinted, determined to see something, the less I saw.

If I had seen someone, it was most definitely Nancy: I recognised the way she held herself.

Something inside me convinced me to walk away, to think nothing of it. For now. Begrudgingly, I obeyed, returning quietly back indoors and back to bed. Equally, there I felt a strange affirmation in how that place was indeed the location of my nightly visits.

Without need of further sleep, I watched sunlight bleed through salt-smeared windows. The backdoor creaked open. It shook me alert and I refrained from moving. I immediately closed my eyes, listening. Although I was already certain I spied her in the abandoned hut, this only reinforced it as I heard her shuffle indoors.

I heard the back-door latch gently click in place, the snap-crack of a floorboard, then a pause, and finally the slight creak of the bedroom door as it closed.

I remained awake, thinking about everything, and concluding with nothing, until both George and Nancy emerged in what then became a normal morning. Although, it may very well have been my imagination, I was convinced Nancy eyed me in a particularly curious way. There was no sign of that familiar hatred, more suspicion.

In return, I was suspicious of her. She was spending time at the derelict hut. As was I.

To what end?

The day continued as usual and I spent most of the time on the beach staring out to sea. Every time I thought about *things*, the hut, Nancy, my dreams, I was aware that my fingers drifted to the lump at the back of my head, the now-healed wound.

Later indoors, when George was still repairing the damage to his boat, I was left with Nancy's scowl for company. All the while I sensed she wanted to say something. Strangely, I was not disappointed when she soon confronted me.

She sat at the table stitching George's tunic.

"You've been there, haven't you?" she said.

"Been where?" I knew where she meant, I knew precisely what she was asking.

"To the old hut, farther along the beach." She stood and approached me, pulling her shawl tighter over her shoulders.

A heat rose to my face. I knew I had been outside during most nights – perhaps I had visited the derelict hut, perhaps I walked there in my sleep … Perhaps … And then I knew without doubt that was precisely where I was going every night.

She gripped her shawl tight, glaring down at me.

"You have! Don't lie to me!"

She knew, just as I, that I had indeed visited the abandoned hut. Not only had it been a place of shelter after I came ashore, but there was undoubtedly more to that place. So much more.

I kept my lips pressed together, clenching my jaw and feeling the reassuring presence warm my head, my entire body.

"Never go there again. Ever."

I felt my toes twitch as though she somehow saw residue of that tar-like substance.

She went back to the table and picked up George's tunic. All the while throwing the occasional challenging glance.

The rest of the evening was spent in near silence as it often was when just the two of us remained indoors. Little did I know it then, but when George returned and we ate a meal of fish and potato, it would be the final time the three of us would share something so normal.

***

That night, I startled awake. Only this time I discovered I was not in my bed. Nor was I even in the cottage. Instead I was outside, and suspected like many a night previous I had walked there in my sleep.

To what end, I would soon discover.

There was a saltiness on my lips and I wiped it away.

A loose plank rocked in the wind, repeatedly slapping the wall as though to demand my attention. I was sprawled across the threshold of the abandoned hut. I slowly sat up and pulled my over-sized tunic tight around me. The haze of moonlight pressed down on swirling fog that shrouded the beach. I shifted position and squinted into the shadows of the hut. A pungency of vegetation forced itself into my lungs. It was laced with something heavier: decay. Rotten floorboards glistened in the moonlight. The tall grass which had before protruded in a corner had become a dusty heap of straw. Moisture dripped from overhead rafters, and the brambles were now nothing more than shrivelled twists. Boards creaked as I shuffled and crawled farther inside, enough to remove myself from the chill wind.

Nearby something shifted under the floorboards, more a slurping noise. I eyed the scattered debris. A peculiar growth of vegetation had risen through a broken section of boards to spread up the timber wall. It had fused with a fishing net. Another sound, this time outside: clacking pebbles. Someone approached from the other side of the hut.

My fingers slid through the dense matter that covered the wall as I moved deeper into the gloom. I shrank into a corner, now embraced by shadows, unsurprised to recognise the same curious substance discovered on numerous occasions. Whatever it was inside me, this thing that was more a presence, requested my simple acceptance. I attempted to silence my breath which now came out in short gasps, and seemed only to accentuate a hammering heartbeat.

Then a voice: "I knew it!"

It was Nancy. Dressed in nightclothes and wrapped in her shawl, she leaned through the hole in the opposite wall. It was as though I relived my arrival to Dungeness, after the sinking of the *Josephine Willis*.

"What are you doing?" she demanded.

Near my head there again was that sucking noise and instead of unnerving me, I found it reassuring.

"Get out of there!" she yelled.

Pressing my palms to the soft boards, fingers sliding in the vegetative growth, I steadied myself to stand. Nancy sucked air through clenched teeth and stooped to fully enter the hut. I stood, and something tickled the hair at the back of my skull.

And finally … *finally* I understood.

I grinned and took pleasure in seeing how her eyes widened, and I read doubt on her pinched face.

"How dare you, boy!" Those words at another time would have stung, yet now fell into the shadows as though absorbed.

I knew why I had woken there. I knew that I had been coming to the hut these past few weeks, every night to tend to … something. A brief pain speared the back of my head, albeit now familiar. There was something else here, beneath the floorboards. And it belonged to me. I recalled what I had witnessed the night of my arrival, when taking shelter there in the hut. I recalled how I had seen her shift the wooden boards back in place.

"I know what you did," I told her.

Again, there was doubt in her eyes. Even though the surrounding gloom was as thick as the fog outside, I recognised the way she looked deflated. I crouched and with a strength surprising even to me, I pulled up one of the planks and cast it aside.

"Stop it," she said.

I bent and hooked up another, then stepped towards her. For the first time I felt in charge of the situation.

"Leave," she said without looking at me. "Now."

"No."

Then she did look up. Her eyes glistened. "What?"

"I said: no."

A noise from outside made us both look round, to squint out into the fog.

It was George.

"What is this?" His voice was firm yet contained an edge of fear. "Nancy? Sydney?"

Nancy was about to say something when George groaned, deep in his throat. Mouth downturned, he slowly shook his head. I took another step forward and saw what was hidden beneath the floorboards. My breath snatched in my throat. That voice, that presence deep within, that *something* which had been strengthening since surviving the sinking ship, told me I could not be surprised. All this time, I had known what was beneath those boards; I had, after all, been visiting every night guided by that voice to build upon what Nancy kept there.

She, however, had absolutely no idea what I had created.

Not yet.

"Dear ... God!" George bellowed.

His legs folded beneath him and he collapsed beside the missing planks. Nancy shuffled away from him, hitting the timber wall. A board rattled.

"I couldn't bare it," she said. "I wanted my boy back."

George gripped the edge of the boards.

"Nancy, what have you done?"

Two feet lower than the floorboards lay their dead son, William. Only the boy's head was visible while the rest of his body hid in the shadows beneath more boards. His parchment-like skin had stretched taut over the skull, with wrinkled eyelids at the back of sunken sockets. His hair was neat, something no doubt Nancy ensured during every visit. Dirt clung to the strands. She had not yet had a chance to proceed with her usual sad ritual. Not tonight.

George groaned again, like a mewling animal.

"This is unholy," he whispered.

Nancy began weeping.

My hand went to the back of my neck and I probed the small hole just above the hairline.

George's face hardened and slowly stood.

"I'll have none of this," he said and stepped back.

"Please, George," Nancy said between sobs, "I

could not lose my boy."

"Our boy, he was *our* boy."

Nancy suddenly jerked forward and crawled to the edge of the hole. George did not move. He simply held his unlit pipe and looked down at his wife while she hunched over to wail into the very cause of her misery.

"Unholy," he whispered and left the hut.

His heavy footfalls crunched across the pebbles as he hurried away.

"George!" Nancy whimpered through tears that shone in the moonlight. "George, please, George!"

Seeing her cry like that made me feel larger than my years. My hands shook. I felt my muscles tense and I straightened my back. As I heard George stomp away from the hut, I felt a grin spread across my face. I leaned down, and with hands that felt as strong as iron, I gripped a pair of floorboards. Nancy frowned and watched me yank them up. Rusted nails screeched and I threw the boards aside.

She screamed.

Cradled in the slick folds of the vegetation I had harvested, was her son's entire body. Where once he wore clothes, now growths of what could only be described as fungi bulged through the split fabric. It covered his torso, and limbs, and climbed his neck.

Nancy vomited. The stink mixed with the heavy aroma of rotten vegetables and decay.

The sweaty growth beneath the floor rippled in places while in others it shivered. Even now, a section of it swelled and clung to joists, extending with minute slug-like appendages.

A sense of pride in my creation, of what I had

created here, overcame me.

"What... what is this?" Nancy said and wiped her mouth. "What have you done to William?"

Boards creaked as I lunged for her. I snatched at her thin arms and her shawl slipped away. My strength was more than she estimated, and she cried out in shock. She uselessly struggled. The floor splintered beneath our sliding feet and together we sank into the bulging vegetative mass. Its wet warmth enveloped us, welcoming. She released me and flailed, slapping the crusty top layers. Doughy folds seethed and rose up around her.

Immediately I recognised those movements as something akin to that which had lurked beneath the waves while the *Josephine Willis* sank. It had entered my drowned body to bring me back to life. The way it moved was similar, although this was much larger and was to feed the thing inside me.

I watched in awe as the shivering layers of vegetation bubbled and split wide, slurping as it took Nancy down. I allowed the warm folds to cradle me while I watched it smother her. On the instant her scream escalated into panic, it forced itself into her mouth. She choked, her eyes wide, and she sank. Her hair draped across the surface, churning with the bubbling layers, and eventually vanished.

Soon, the rippling folds settled.

I inhaled that sweet aroma of sulphur and salt. Regardless of my new strength and sharpened senses, I still had only a 12-year-old's body and so found it awkward to climb out. The vegetation seemed to clutch at me as I lifted myself clear. With breath sharp in my lungs, I sat on the edge of the boards and closed my eyes. The hole in the back of my neck tingled and a cool sensation travelled down my spine.

The sound of pebbles beneath heavy boots broke the quiet, and George returned. He held a can of oil and some rags.

"I need to burn this," he said as he stopped on the threshold, "before anyone—" He squinted into the gloom and saw his wife's discarded shawl. "Where is she?"

I stood. "Please. Let's go home."

"Sydney?"

I deliberately halted his approach, knowing he must not be allowed to burn that which I had created. To hide any confidence, I relaxed my face.

"Nancy didn't mean to upset you." I wrapped slick arms around his leg.

"Where did she go?"

Although satisfied he was unable to get any farther inside I gripped tighter. From where he stood, clutching the pyro materials, I assumed he did not want to look at his dead son. In doing so, I doubted he even realised I had exposed more of the body. I certainly did not want him to see, let alone burn the evidence of his wife's mad deceit. I wanted everything to return to normal: just the two of us. Now with Nancy out of the way, perhaps …

It was my turn to groan. I knew it to be impossible, how things could never be the same.

George tried to step closer, holding the can away from my head. The smell of oil was strong, and it stung my nostrils. I clamped his leg tighter.

"Sydney, let go."

"Please, no."

"I must do this."

"I want to go back home." I squeezed that much more.

His eyes widened, evidently surprised at my strength, but still he took another step forward, closer to my own secret. I knew I was just as bad as Nancy in that respect.

"No, George, please."

I thought of how this man had taken me into their home despite his wife's reluctance. I thought of his love, so evident especially in those moments away from Nancy's spiteful eyes. And the driftwood ship he made and had been heartlessly burned. Here we were. More fire to hand.

I could not let this happen.

The warmth at the back of my neck spread out and around me, filling me, channelling around my body. This time not just to my arms and hands and fingers, not only to my legs and feet and toes, but now it surged inwards, deep, to the core of my 12-year-old self. It was then that I knew I would remain there, in that body, stunted and dependant on the very crop I had harvested. And I would do it alone.

I released George's leg to look up at him. In turn, he looked down upon me. Tears blurred my vision.

And I shoved him … to join his wife and son.

The slurping and sucking noises began instantly.

I stumbled away, unable to watch. Those sounds echoed as I strolled from the hut, and soon faded. Eventually I staggered into the cottage. A coldness spread through me and I collapsed onto the mattress, face down. I reached underneath the bed and my numbed fingers pulled out the charred remains of the driftwood ship. I pressed it to my chest, though felt only a chilling and aching heaviness. And there was that spreading heat from the back of my neck, soothing, reassuring, promising. Whether primordial or indeed something not of this Earth it was a comfort.

Alone in the home that would be mine for many years to come, I clutched the blackened ship. The tears flowed.

It had already begun, though I believe at that moment the thing inside me strengthened immeasurably and granted me a longevity to this day I wonder if I deserve.

Also from Mark Cassell

Dungeness, Britain's only desert and one of Europe's largest expanses of shingle... and where surviving the harvest is the easy part.

Twelve-year-old Sydney often looks out across the ocean, recalling the night in which the ship sank. He still tastes the salt water that stole his life over one hundred and fifty years ago.

Cane and Jo visit Dungeness, combining a family reunion with a house hunt. Not only do they discover two generations of secrets, they also unearth a local horror beneath the shingle beach.

When the lives of Sydney and the couple entwine, the crop has other ideas about the true meaning of happily ever after.

Surviving the harvest is the easy part...

https://www.markcassell.co.uk/parasite-crop

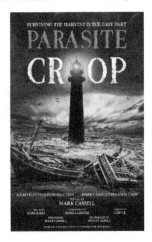

From Mark Cassell, author of the Shadow Fabric mythos, comes *SIX!*

A unique collection of dark tales, featuring:
SKIN
Hypodermic needles, a tattoo machine, and screams... there are many secrets in this married couple's basement.
ALL IN THE EYES
Grandmothers should be generous, share unconditional love and bake cookies, right? Not this one.
IN LOVING MEMORY
Lightning strikes twice. Once during the mischief of an eleven-year-old boy, and the second as an adult when least expected.
THE SPACE BETWEEN SPACES
A gothic account of the peculiar events leading up to Edgar Allan Poe's untimely death.
ON SET WITH NORTH
When an actor invites his driving instructor on set they soon question the special effects.
DON'T SWEAR IN MUM'S HOUSE
Two siblings clear out their family home only to disturb more than memories.

https://mybook.to/Six

Also from Red Cape Publishing

Anthologies:

Short Story Collections:

Embrace the Darkness by P.J. Blakey-Novis
Tunnels by P.J. Blakey-Novis
The Artist by P.J. Blakey-Novis
Karma by P.J. Blakey-Novis
The Place Between Worlds by P.J. Blakey-Novis
Home by P.J. Blakey-Novis
Short Horror Stories by P.J. Blakey-Novis
Short Horror Stories Vol.2 by P.J. Blakey-Novis
Keep It Inside & Other Weird Tales by Mark Anthony Smith
Everything's Annoying by J.C. Michael
Old Tales Reborn by J.C. Michael
Six! By Mark Cassell
Six! Volume 2 by Mark Cassell
Monsters in the Dark by Donovan 'Monster' Smith
Barriers by David F. Gray
Love & Other Dead Things by Astrid Addams
Bone Carver by Gemma Paul
Shadows of Death by Dee Caples

Novelettes:

The Ivory Tower by Antoinette Corvo
By His Hand by William R. Perry

Novellas:

Four by P.J. Blakey-Novis
Dirges in the Dark by Antoinette Corvo
The Cat That Caught the Canary by Antoinette Corvo
Bow-Legged Buccaneers from Outer Space by David Owain Hughes
Spiffing by Tim Mendees
A Splintered Soul by Adrian Meredith
Scavengers of the Sun by Adrian Meredith

Novels:

Madman Across the Water by Caroline Angel
The Curse Awakens by Caroline Angel
Less by Caroline Angel
Where Shadows Move by Caroline Angel
Origin of Evil by Caroline Angel
Origin of Evil: Beginnings by Caroline Angel
Exist by Caroline Angel
The Vegas Rift by David F. Gray
The Broken Doll by P.J. Blakey-Novis
The Broken Doll: Shattered Pieces by P.J. Blakey-Novis
South by Southwest Wales by David Owain Hughes
Any Which Way but South Wales by David Owain Hughes
All Roads Lead to South Wales by David Owain Hughes
Appletown by Antoinette Corvo
Nails by K.J. Sargeant
The Eternal by Timothy Friesenhahn
Lead Me to the Dark by James Twyman

Art Books:

Demons Never Die by David Paul Harris & P.J. Blakey-Novis
Six Days of Violence by P.J Blakey-Novis & David Paul Harris

Magazines:

Cauldron of Chaos

Follow Red Cape Publishing

www.redcapepublishing.com
www.facebook.com/redcapepublishing
www.twitter.com/redcapepublish
www.instagram.com/redcapepublishing
www.pinterest.co.uk/redcapepublishing
www.patreon.com/redcapepublishing
www.ko-fi.com/redcape
www.buymeacoffee.com/redcape

Printed in Great Britain
by Amazon

23285158R00076